Her Amish Chaperone

Leigh Bale

LOVE INSPIRED
INSPIRATIONAL ROMANCE

LOVE INSPIRED®
INSPIRATIONAL ROMANCE

Recycling programs for this product may not exist in your area.

ISBN-13: 978-1-335-48829-9

Her Amish Chaperone

Copyright © 2020 by Lora Lee Bale

This edition published by arrangement with Harlequin Books S.A.

For questions and comments about the quality of this book, please contact us at CustomerService@Harlequin.com.

Love Inspired
22 Adelaide St. West, 40th Floor
Toronto, Ontario M5H 4E3, Canada
www.Harlequin.com

Printed in U.S.A.

Peace I leave with you, my peace I give unto you: not as the world giveth, give I unto you. Let not your heart be troubled, neither let it be afraid.

—*John* 14:27

This book is dedicated to Shana Asaro,
Melissa Endlich and Diane Parkinson.
Thank you for supporting and believing in me.
You transformed my heart and mind
and made me a better writer.

Chapter One

Caroline Schwartz didn't dare take her eyes off her feet. If she did, she knew she'd fall flat on her face. At the age of nineteen, she should be able to run past this crosswalk on Main Street without even thinking about it. But after the buggy accident that nearly took her life, it was amazing she could walk at all.

Thankfully, there wasn't much traffic in the sleepy farming town of Riverton, Colorado. Caroline's progress was slow. She gripped the handles of her elbow crutches and inched forward, taking several shuffling steps. The plastic sack of pencils and notepads she'd just purchased from the general store swung easily from her fingers. Pressing her tongue against the roof of her mouth, she concentrated on every step and vowed she would one day do this again without the aid of crutches.

Ignoring her aching muscles and joints, she lifted her feet higher. The black asphalt emanated heat she could feel even through her plain Amish shoes. But she didn't mind. At least it wasn't snowing. She welcomed the dry August sunshine that beat down on her white organdy prayer *kapp*.

The accident last January had crushed her pelvis and broken both her legs. And what had followed had been a long, depressing winter. She'd spent several months in the hospital with her legs and hips in traction, followed by weeks of excruciating physical therapy. The doctors hadn't given her much hope of walking again, but she'd proved them wrong. Ignoring the screaming pain, she'd diligently pushed herself to stand and move her legs. Finally, she'd graduated to elbow crutches. And walking across the street today on her own power was a tremendous victory. It meant she could resume her teaching assignment at the Amish school next month and wouldn't be a burden on her *familye* any longer.

It meant freedom and independence.

The narrow sidewalk extended past the general store but ended just a few feet beyond the post office. If she could make it there, her aunt Hannah would help her to the buggy. Caroline had insisted on walking to the store alone today, but she was tired now and desperately needed to sit down.

The sudden blaring of a horn startled her and she jerked her head up. Two glass headlights and the shiny silver grill of a brand-new black pickup truck stood no more than twenty inches away. She lifted her gaze higher and saw Rand Henbury glaring at her from behind the tinted windshield. Rand was the eighteen-year-old son of the richest *Englisch* rancher in the area. Two of his *Englisch* friends sat in the truck beside him.

Vroom! Vroom!

Rand revved the engine impatiently and honked the

horn again. In her haste to get out of the way, Caroline lost her balance and tumbled to the ground in a giant heap. Her crutches clattered around her and she cried out as small rocks dug into her knees and the palms of her hands. As she struggled to push herself up, she heard Rand and his friends' raucous laughter.

A feeling of absolute fear coursed through Caroline's veins. The night of the buggy accident rushed over her in dizzying horror. With perfect clarity, she recalled every sickening sound of smashing wood and the screeching of her broken horse. When help finally arrived, the poor animal had to be put down. And when she'd awoken in the hospital, Caroline had been beyond grateful they didn't shoot people, because her body was just as shattered.

Not twenty minutes before the car struck her buggy, she'd seen the driver yelling and throwing things in the general store. Such a temper was alien to Caroline and her Amish people. They were pacifists, adhering to Jesus Christ's teachings to turn the other cheek no matter what. She'd hurried to her buggy and was on her way home when the man had come upon her in his car. Because he'd been in a drunken rage, he'd been driving too fast and couldn't stop his vehicle in time. But Caroline had learned firsthand why anger and violence were to be shunned. And even though it had happened eight months earlier, it felt like it was happening all over again. Right now.

"Schtopp! Waard e bissel."

She heard the *Deitsch* words behind her but couldn't turn to see who was speaking. Strong hands lifted her and she stared into the face of Benjamin Yoder, her

Amish bishop's recalcitrant nephew from Iowa. As she faced her rescuer, Caroline wasn't sure if she should be grateful or even more frightened.

Rumor haunted Ben's name. Hushed whispers claimed he had killed a man seven years earlier. That was why he'd moved here to Colorado. To escape his dark past. And though he was a member in good standing of the *Gmay*, her Amish community here in Riverton, she couldn't trust him. Not ever.

"I have you. It'll be all right now." His deep voice sounded soft, sympathetic and soothing.

He spoke in *Deitsch*, the language of their people. And as he carried her across the street, Caroline felt absolutely safe in his arms. Then she reminded herself who he was and who she was—and she wanted away from him as fast as possible.

With her out of the road, Rand revved the engine of his truck and surged forward. The vehicle accelerated, disappearing around the corner with a squealing of brakes and a smattering of gravel.

Breathing hard, Caroline had no choice but to wrap her arms around Ben's neck. He carried her as if she were light as a baby bird. Beneath her hands, she felt the bunching of his solid muscles and remembered all the stories that surrounded his name.

Violent! Killer!

He was everything Caroline loathed. She'd heard all the gossip. Standing at six feet four inches tall, Ben weighed around two hundred pounds, all of it muscle. He was large and strong and Bishop Yoder called him Big Ben, with good reason. Though everyone in their Amish community kept their distance, the men included

Ben in their work projects because he had the strength and stamina of three men. But he never complained. In fact, he was inordinately quiet and kept mostly to himself. He'd become an asset to their *Gmay*, especially when they were building a new house or barn. But just like the drunk driver who had struck Caroline's buggy and almost killed her, she believed Ben had a foul temper. And she wanted nothing to do with a man like him. No, nothing at all.

As Ben reached the sidewalk, she caught his open expression. He was ruggedly handsome, with a lean jaw and blunt, stubborn chin. His nose was slightly crooked, as if it had been broken before. Though she was almost as afraid of this man as she was of Rand Henbury, she saw nothing in Ben's gaze but sympathy and concern.

"Please don't tell the bishop about this. Please!" she whispered to him, fearing she might be deemed incapable and lose her teaching position at the Amish school.

Ben met her gaze, a sober expression on his face. And then he did something that caused her to catch her breath. He winked.

"As you wish. Don't worry. It'll be our little secret," he said.

She stared at him, stunned from the top of her head to the tips of her toes. Did he really mean it?

"Caroline!" Aunt Hannah called.

Too late! Aunt Hannah and Sarah Yoder, the bishop's wife, came running out of the post office. Cliff Packer, the town's *Englisch* postmaster, joined them. No doubt they'd all seen what had happened. There would be no way to keep it secret now.

"Geht es dir gut?" Sarah asked.

"*Ja*, I'm all right. There's nothing to worry about," Caroline reassured them all, but her voice wobbled slightly.

"What happened?" Aunt Hannah asked.

Caroline tapped Ben's sturdy shoulder. "Please, put me down."

He did so, setting her on a wooden bench. As he drew his large hands away, she was cognizant of his promise. Too many people had seen what had happened to keep it private, but she was impressed that Ben had been willing to try. And though she knew he was prone to violence, she wondered if he was a man of his word.

He stood back, not saying anything. His straw hat shaded his clean-shaven face, and she could no longer see his expression. He looped his thumbs through the black suspenders crisscrossing his blue chambray shirt, looking like the very tall, plain Amish man he was. And yet, Caroline sensed there was so much more to Ben Yoder than what she'd been told. Though her senses were on high alert, her curiosity demanded she know more about his past. To understand what was behind his quiet exterior. What had made him angry enough to kill another human being? But she wouldn't ask. For one thing, it wasn't her business. And for another, never again could she take chances with her life. She wanted away from Ben. And fast.

"Can we please go home now?" she asked her aunt.

Hannah picked up the two crutches, her face creased with a stern frown. "Of course. I told you it was too soon for you to go traipsing off around town on your own. You should have let me accompany you to the store. I don't see how you'll be able to teach school this year. You still need lots of help."

The scolding stung. But Caroline knew her aunt meant well. Hannah was a kind woman and her words stemmed from fear, not cruelty. Over the past months of Caroline's rehabilitation, Aunt Hannah had been there for her all the way, without a single murmur of complaint. And it was because of her aunt that she even had a teaching position here in Riverton at all. They'd both come from Ohio and had always been quite close.

But although Caroline laughed off her aunt's concerns, she had her own misgivings. She still couldn't walk very well and wondered how she could effectively teach the Amish children on her own. Back east, there were many children packed into each Amish parochial school, so they usually had at least two teachers. But that wasn't the case here in Colorado where the Amish community was quite small. They only had one teacher and Caroline was it. No wonder the bishop had told her the day before that he was going to assign an assistant to help her. But she wasn't happy at all when he informed her that her new assistant was going to be Ben Yoder.

"Don't worry so much. The *kinder* will be there to help me. And I'm gaining in strength every day." Caroline spoke with a confidence she didn't completely feel. She hated the thought of relying on a man like Ben to chop firewood and clear snow from the paths. But she really had no choice. Not unless she wanted to defy the bishop and school board, which she would never do.

"But what if you fall in the classroom?" Aunt Hannah asked.

"Then I'll pick myself up just like I do at home," Caroline replied, omitting the fact that at home, she could crawl over to a wall or table to brace herself against as she got to her knees and then stood. She'd have to do the same at school. But that could be a problem during recess, when she was outside with no walls to offer support.

"I saw everything!" Cliff Packer exclaimed. "Rand threatened to run her over. He and his friends cause trouble for everyone in town. They shoplift and vandalize our stores and hassle our customers. I can call the police, if you like. This should be reported."

"That won't be necessary. We're leaving town now. No harm was done." Sarah Yoder spoke briskly, taking Aunt Hannah's arm.

Caroline wasn't surprised the bishop's wife rejected Cliff's offer. Her people shunned contention of any kind. As pacifists, they would never fight back, nor would they sue anyone in a court of law. It wasn't their way. The last thing they wanted right now was to call the police.

"Rand and his friends zip around the county roads and terrorize the Amish in the area, too. The bishop should be told. Maybe he'll decide it's finally time to talk to the police about it." Aunt Hannah spoke in *Deitsch*, so Cliff couldn't understand her words.

"I don't know what the police can do. You know Amos has spoken to the boy's *vadder* before and he wouldn't listen," Sarah said.

"*Ach*, please don't tell the bishop. Please!" Caroline begged, knowing they would never make a vow of silence the way Ben had.

"But Caroline, we have to tell him," Sarah said.

"He doesn't need to know," she continued. "People fall all the time. And it certainly doesn't impact my ability to teach. As many times as I fall down, the *gut* Lord will give me the strength to get back up."

But even as she said the words, Caroline knew Sarah would run right home and tell her husband everything that had transpired. By tomorrow morning everyone in her community would know about it, both Amish and *Englisch*.

Hopefully, the bishop and the other two school board members wouldn't care. They knew what she'd been through this past year and how hard she'd worked to rehabilitate herself. She desperately wanted to keep her job. She needed to believe that she was worth something and could benefit her community. That she wasn't just a burden to everyone around her. After all, she could never marry now. Not after what had happened to her.

She turned away and blinked back tears of grief, resolved not to give in to the discouragement. Out of her peripheral vision, she caught Ben's steady gaze. He watched her quietly, as if he could see deep inside her heart. Surely, he had heard all the gossip about her, too. Including how she'd lost much more than just the use of her legs in that horrible accident. She'd also lost her ability to have children. And what Amish man would want her now? The Amish cherished large families. Children meant everything to them. Even if she could find a man to love her for who she was, she could never marry him. Not when she knew she could never give him the kids he would undoubtedly want.

Instead, she must be content with being a teacher. Over time, she would settle into a routine. She would work and live her entire life in this community, but she was determined to pay her own way. She'd almost lost her life and ability to walk. She couldn't lose her career, too. Her job gave her a reason to get up every morning. To keep trying. That was all she needed.

She was determined to return to the classroom and love the children she taught as if they were her own. It would be enough to ease the ache in her heart. It must be! Because the alternative was to become an invalid and spend the rest of her life with bitterness and loneliness as her constant companions. And she was not willing to accept that. No way, no how.

"Ben, will you carry Caroline to our buggy, please? I fear she's too worn out to walk there by herself now," Aunt Hannah said in a polite tone.

Ben looked up, startled by the request. "Of course."

Realizing Caroline was in no condition to walk on her own, he nodded and reached out to scoop her into his arms. As he did so, he caught the uncertain look in her wide eyes. The fear and dread.

Looking away, he carried her the short distance to the parking lot where an open-air cover and hitching posts had been erected by the town for the Amish to use. He tried to ignore the pounding in his heart. If their two aunts hadn't witnessed what had happened, he would have kept his promise to Caroline. He would have kept the incident a secret to his dying day. But now it appeared that everyone in the *Gmay* would soon hear all about it. No doubt the *Englischers* in their community would, too.

"I'm so sorry about this." Caroline spoke so softly that he almost didn't hear.

Her apology hit him hard. "You have nothing to be sorry about."

And he meant it. Through no fault of her own, she needed his help. And he was happy to be of service. The bishop, his uncle, had spoken to him about her situation last night, just after he'd returned from informing Caroline that the school board had assigned Ben to tend to her and the needs of the school this year. From her sour expression, Ben figured she wasn't happy to be saddled with him. But she had no choice.

Until she could walk and get along well on her own, Ben was to put aside his regular farm work with his uncle and focus entirely on Caroline and the school. The bishop and his sons would assume Ben's chores for the time being, but that wasn't the biggest problem here. Caroline was strong-willed and independent. No doubt she didn't want him hanging around her all the time. But more than that, Ben sensed she was afraid of him. He could see it in her eyes every time she looked at him. Surely, she'd heard the gossip surrounding his name and thought he was a dangerous man. And she was dead right.

"Everything's going to be okay." He spoke just as softly, wishing he could believe his own words. But he knew what she must think of him.

Killer. Murderer. It's what he thought of himself, too.

"I hope you're right," she said.

He looked away, not knowing what else to say. His parents had died when he was young. As an only child, he'd been taken in by one of his uncles in a small farming community in Iowa. By the time he was a teenager, he'd grown to a great height and had learned to work hard and love *Gott*. But more than anything else in the world, he wanted a *familye* of his own. A wife and children to shower his love upon. To the Amish, *familye* meant everything. But for Ben, it was even more personal. If he had a *familye* of his own, it would help make up for what he'd lost with his parents. Give him a sense of belonging. A woman and kids to spend the rest of his life with would be his dream come true. But in his heart, he knew it was futile.

He'd killed a man with his bare hands. No good Amish woman would ever marry him now.

He set Caroline in her buggy and stepped away. He saw the flutter of her lashes as she looked down. She made a pretense of tucking several strands of golden hair back inside her white prayer *kapp* before straightening her white apron and long, burgundy dress. She glanced up and he saw her true feelings emblazoned in her beautiful blue eyes. Distrust. Fear. Repulsion. They were all there, plain as the small, upturned nose on her face.

She didn't speak but looked away. He gazed at her pretty profile for several moments, feeling mesmerized. Since the day he'd first seen her in church, he'd thought she was the most amazing woman he'd ever met. She had a smooth, creamy complexion any woman would envy and delicate eyebrows that arched perfectly over her eyes. But jealousy wasn't part of the Amish faith. In fact, his people rejected *Hochmut*, the pride of men. And because of how demure she was, Ben doubted Caroline was even aware how lovely she was.

As she folded her hands in her lap, he got the feeling her movements were contrived so she could avoid speaking to him again. And he didn't blame her one bit. With his reputation, he wouldn't want to be friends with him, either.

"*Danke*, Ben. I'm so grateful you were here today." Hannah broke into his thoughts.

He nodded, stepping back several paces. "It was my pleasure. I'm glad I could help out."

Without a backward glance, Hannah hurried to the driver's seat and took the leather lead lines into her practiced grip. She didn't say another word as she slapped them against the horse's back.

"Haw!" she called and the buggy jerked forward.

"You take care and travel safely." Sarah waved as she called after her and Caroline.

Hannah gave a curt nod.

"*Komm* on. Let's go *heemet*." Sarah touched Ben's elbow as she hurried toward their own horse and buggy tethered a short distance away.

"*Ja*, I'll take you home." He nodded his assent and followed, ensuring that all her packages were stowed safely in the back. Then he climbed into the driver's seat.

As he drove them home, he couldn't help thinking about the past. The legal system had ruled the killing as self-defense and he hadn't faced any jail time. But that didn't matter to Ben. Even though it happened seven years earlier, he still couldn't forget. Couldn't get the awful scene out of his heart and mind. He'd taken another human life, and it haunted him day and night.

"Just wait until your *onkel* Amos hears about this. I

don't know what he'll say. I'm sure he'll be upset. Rand Henbury has made it so none of us dare venture into town to do our shopping or even drive our *kinder* to school. We never know when that *Englisch* boy might come upon us and terrorize us with that awful truck of his." Sarah sat beside him, staring out the windshield, shaking her head.

Yes, Uncle Amos would be mighty upset by the news. Ben's uncle was the bishop of the Amish *Gmay* here in Riverton and had a duty to protect his flock. He was also a kind man who'd agreed to take Ben into his household. He'd insisted that, if Ben relocated here to Colorado, he could start anew. But Ben had learned differently. Gossip traveled far and wide, and it had followed him here. Everyone in his *Gmay* knew what had happened to him back in Iowa, and they didn't want anything to do with him, either.

The quick clopping of the horse's hooves on the asphalt built an urgency inside Ben. What if Rand Henbury was still driving along the county road and came upon Caroline and her aunt as they made their way home? Rand might hassle them again and upset Caroline even worse.

"Haw!" Ben hurried his horse into a faster trot, hoping to catch up to them. He wanted to ensure they got home safely.

Within minutes he saw their black buggy just ahead. The fluorescent slow-moving-vehicle symbol on the back gleamed in the morning sunlight. It swayed back and forth as a reminder for automobiles to slow down, but many drivers ignored the caution. Some were busy texting or talking on their cell phones and ran right over the Amish. No wonder they had so many buggy accidents. Many drivers were too inattentive and in too big a hurry. The town had started putting up cautionary signs along the roads, but it didn't seem to help much.

The bishop's farm was only a mile past the turnoff to the Schwartz's place. When the buggy Caroline was traveling in turned off the county road and headed toward their home, Ben breathed a sigh of relief. They were on the stretch of dirt that led directly to their farm. Rand wouldn't bother them now. In just a few more minutes Ben would have his aunt Sarah home safe, too.

As they pulled off the main road, Sarah breathed a heavy sigh. "I'm not sure Caroline is really up to teaching right now. I think she needs another year to recover from her accident. I'm glad your *onkel* and the school board decided to assign you to drive her wherever she needs to go and to work at the school. They feared that making her wait another year to teach might break her morale. She's already lost so much. All she has left is that teaching job. Poor Caroline."

Yes, poor Caroline. Ben remembered what she was like before the accident. Confident, vivacious and happy. The single Amish men from miles around had flocked to her side, vying for her hand in marriage. But not him. He had nothing to offer her except a tainted reputation. With her sweet nature and pretty face, she could marry anyone she wanted. As a proper Amish girl, she wouldn't be caught dead riding around with a savage man like him. In fact, he was surprised the bishop would assign him to accompany her wherever she needed to go. Being near him could sully her reputation. But with the bishop's sanction, no one would dare challenge him. Not even Caroline. So she was pretty much stuck with him, whether she liked it or not.

"Once the bad weather sets in, she'll need your help more than ever. And until she can walk better, you'll even have to drive her to and from school," Sarah continued.

Ben nodded but didn't speak. He wasn't surprised that Sarah knew about his new task. Last night the bishop had explained in great detail what he wanted him to do. Ben just hoped Caroline wasn't overly upset about the assignment.

"This might be just what the two of you need. You've both been hurt and seem like kindred spirits. With all the time you'll be spending together, maybe you can become *gut* friends," Sarah said, her voice filled with hope.

Ben forced himself not to laugh out loud. He doubted Caroline would ever consider him a friend. Not if he was the last person on earth.

They drove past the one-room schoolhouse, a red log building that inhabited one corner of the bishop's eastern hay field. All of the Amish fathers had built the house from a kit they'd ordered from a local manufacturer here in Colorado. The schoolyard included a spacious dirt area where the kids could play baseball outside. An outhouse stood in the back, along with a small barn for stabling ponies and horses until the children were ready to go home in the afternoon. And twining past the property, the sparkling waters of Grape Creek glimmered in the sunlight with clutches of wild purple iris and cattails growing along the grassy embankments.

It was a lovely place to go to school, though it definitely needed some playground equipment. They'd recently purchased a swing set, teeter-totter and tether ball equipment, and it would be one of Ben's jobs to put it all together and install it securely on the playground. At least he'd have something to do during the daytime while he waited to accompany Caroline home each afternoon.

Ben thought about how different Caroline had been since the accident that had interrupted her teaching career last year. Gone was the confident gleam in her eyes. Instead of walking with a bounce in her stride, she could barely shuffle across the street without getting run over. He was happy to help her. Though he'd come here to flee his shadowed past, he had deserved what he got. But not Caroline. She'd done nothing to deserve the angst and pain she'd been forced to suffer.

"Are you *allrecht*?" Sarah asked as they pulled into the graveled driveway of his uncle's farmyard.

"*Ja*, why do you ask?"

She laid a hand on his arm and met his gaze. "I know how hard life has been for you since you lost your parents, Ben. I'm sure what happened to Caroline today has upset you, too. But remember to turn the other cheek. It's what Jesus taught us to do. If you trust in *Gott*, everything will work out fine. You just need to have faith."

Hmm. If only it were that easy.

With one last pat on his hand, Sarah turned and climbed out of the buggy. As she walked toward the house, Ben stared after her, feeling a bit shocked by her words. Did she think he might retaliate against Rand Henbury for what he'd done to Caroline today?

Of course he wouldn't. He knew vengeance belonged to *Gott* alone. It would profit him nothing to retaliate against Rand. And yet, because of Ben's past, people still doubted him. One big mistake had almost ruined his entire life.

As he drove the horse to the barn and unhitched the animal from the buggy, Ben's mind was filled with turmoil. Both him and Caroline were victims of violence. She'd been treated brutally and now was struggling to recover from what someone else had done to her. And Ben had become that which his people detested more than anything else. A brute. A killer of the most heinous kind.

He'd been taught from his youth to turn the other cheek. But he'd failed. And now he silently yearned for redemption. If only God could forgive him for what he'd done.

If only he could forgive himself.

Chapter Two

The week before school started, Caroline coordinated a work project. Morning sunshine gleamed warm and bright as Aunt Hannah pulled the buggy into the graveled schoolyard. Sitting beside her with a broom and bucket of cleaning supplies, Caroline smiled with satisfaction. A number of the mothers were already there to meet them, including Sarah Yoder, Norma Albrecht, Linda Hostetler and Becca Graber, the young woman who had substituted at the school last year while Caroline was in the hospital. The temporary assignment had proven to be a blessing for Becca. She had met her future husband, Jesse King, when she had been tutoring his young son, Sam. The two had fallen in love and would soon wed in late November. Caroline wished something that amazing might happen to her but doubted she'd ever be so blessed.

"*Ach*, it looks like you've got a *gut* cleaning crew ready to work. This project shouldn't take us very long," Aunt Hannah said as she directed the horse and buggy around back where she parked.

Caroline was pleased by the turnout. They'd sweep and dust the school and be finished before lunchtime. She might even have time to hang the new alphabet symbols around the room, along with some Amish proverbs she'd written out on poster board.

Looking up, she saw Ben Yoder standing at the back woodpile, and a tense feeling blanketed her.

"I still don't know why he has to be here," Caroline said beneath her breath.

Aunt Hannah shrugged. "The bishop explained all of that to you. The school board wants him to assist you until you're back on your feet."

"I am on my feet," she grumbled, gesturing to her black practical shoes.

"Not very well. You fall easily and can't lift much yet. Give yourself time. And until then, Ben is here to help," Hannah said.

Her aunt's candor didn't make the situation any easier. Yes, Caroline knew the bishop's reasoning and understood what he wanted, but she still couldn't accept it. She didn't want Ben Yoder here—it was that simple.

She gestured to her elbow crutches. "I'm slow but I'm walking better every day. I won't need help for very long."

Aunt Hannah made a tsking sound. "Be patient and give yourself time, dear. It's a blessing the bishop and school board have been so considerate of you."

A blessing! Caroline felt it was anything but. Ben would be hanging around all the time, a cloying reminder of the violence that had brought her so much pain.

She pursed her lips to keep from making a derogatory comment, her gaze returning to Ben. He was busy with his chore and had no idea she was watching him. Because it was still summertime, he wore a plain straw hat, the long sleeves of his gray shirt rolled up to his elbows. He held an ax in his capable hands and brought the tool down on a small log, splintering it into several chunks of wood.

Whack!

Lodging the blade of the ax head into a large tree stump, he picked up the split pieces of kindling and stacked them tidily in the woodpile. Standing straight, he looked directly at Caroline as she struggled to get her elbow crutches beneath her so she could disembark from the buggy.

"Wait just a minute and I'll help you." Aunt Hannah scurried to get out of the buggy and come around to assist.

Before she knew what was happening, Caroline found two strong hands reaching out to lift her off her seat. Ben didn't linger before setting her on her feet and handing her the crutches. Startled by his speed and strength, Caroline looked up into his dark eyes.

"Guder mariye," Ben said.

"Good morning," she returned, her voice sounding anxious and strained to her ears.

She drew away, leaning on the crutches as she reached for her bookbag and a bucket of cleaning supplies. Ben whisked the bucket out of her hands.

"Here, let me. I can carry it for you," he said.

She pursed her lips together in irritation. "I'm perfectly capable of doing it by myself. These crutches are temporary and I'd like to do what I can without your help."

Okay, not a very charitable thing to say. Ben produced a rather wilted expression and handed the bucket back to her. Caroline took it but felt bad for her stinging remarks. After all, the guy was only trying to help.

"I'm sorry. I didn't mean to be so rude," she said, feeling confused by her own actions. This wasn't like her. She'd never lashed out at anyone like this before. What had gotten into her?

His gaze met hers and he showed a slight smile. It softened his face, making him look quite charming. But she must not forget who this man was and what he'd done. She was not going to become friends with him.

"It's all right. I'm used to it," he said.

Oh, no! That made her feel even worse. She hated to be counted among the people who pushed him away, but she just couldn't get over the fact that Bishop Yoder had forced her to accept this man's help. She didn't want Ben here. She wanted to be left alone. And it rankled her hard that she had no choice in the matter.

"*Ach*, come on, then. We've got work to do." Aunt Hannah headed toward the schoolhouse, carrying a mop and feather duster.

Caroline draped the handle of the bucket over one of her crutch grips and shuffled forward.

"*Hallo!*" the other women greeted them.

"Are you excited to start the new school year?" Becca asked, falling in step beside Caroline.

"I am. Are you excited to get married in a few months?"

Becca nodded, a soft smile curving her lips. "I am. But I'll miss teaching school, too."

"*Ja*, I missed it so much. It feels *gut* to get back to work. I really appreciate you filling in for me after the accident. They might have had to close the school if not for you." Caroline couldn't explain it, but she felt inordinately happy to be here today, even with Ben trailing behind her.

"You're *willkomm*. I was happy to help out. After all, it was this job that led me to my Jesse. I'll always be so grateful that I got to teach here," Becca said.

Caroline smiled. Oh, how she wished she could meet someone who already had children for her to raise, but she knew there would be no happy fairy-tale ending and no ready-made *familye* for her. At least Becca could have children, whereas Caroline could not.

"When are your cousins coming into town?" Sarah asked Hannah.

The group walked slowly toward the schoolhouse, letting Caroline set the pace. They all knew that Hannah's cousin from Ohio was relocating here with her young *familye*. Though she was Caroline's first cousin once removed, she'd known and loved her and her husband all her life. They were friends as well as *familye*.

Caroline absentmindedly listened to the conversation but focused on her steps, conscious of Ben staying close by her side. With so many other people offering to help, she didn't need him here today. She wished he would leave her alone.

"My cousin's name is Anna Bontrager. She and her husband, James, will be here in two weeks and I can hardly wait. They wanted to arrive this week, so their two *kinder* could start school with the other kids, but they just couldn't manage it. It's a lot of work to move all the way from Ohio. They'll be a week late for school, but since they'll be living with us until they can finalize escrow on their own place, Caroline said she could bring the kids up to speed on their schoolwork."

"*Ja*, that is *gut*. How old are the *kinder* again?" Linda asked.

"Mary is five and Seth is six," Hannah said. "Anna is hoping to have another *boppli* next year. And James is planning to buy the old Harlin place. The paperwork is all in order. They just need to get here and sign the final documents."

Caroline made a mental note to include the two new scholars in her lesson plans. It had been several years since she'd seen the children and she doubted they would even remember her. But she knew and loved their parents dearly and looked forward to being with them again. She wanted to make the kids feel welcome and include them in the classroom setup.

"I heard old Mr. Harlin died a while back. And since he had no *kinder* of his own to leave his farm to, the county took it over in a property tax sale," Norma said.

"That's right." Hannah nodded. "Mr. Harlin was *Englisch* and he kept his place in immaculate condition when he was alive. But he's been dead for eleven months now, so his farm has gone to weed and the fields have laid fallow all summer long. James and Anna are getting the house, barn and fields for a very fair price. It includes forty acres of fertile land and it's right next to the bishop's farm."

"So close, isn't that nice? They'll be within walking

distance. I'm sure they'll work hard and make a nice go of the place. Our *Gmay* is really growing. It'll be so *gut* to have them in our community. Amos says new members are the lifeblood of our *Gmay*," Sarah said.

Caroline silently agreed. Back east, the Amish communities were clustered close together and most farms were within walking distance of each other. But here in Colorado, the farms were spread far apart. Getting the children to school each day required extended buggy rides. She was glad her cousins would be living close to her.

They had arrived at the schoolhouse. Standing at the top of the front steps, the women parted the way so Caroline could step forward and unlock the door. As she pulled the shiny silver key out of her bookbag and slid it into the lock, she felt a poignant burst of energy. After the accident, she didn't think she'd ever get to do this again. And here she was, opening the schoolhouse as the teacher. It was a rite of passage for her. A silent signal that she could live and work as a vital member of her community again. If she couldn't marry and have a *familye* of her own, at least she could help raise the other children in her *Gmay*.

Turning the key, she opened the tall oak door and pushed it wide. She hobbled inside, followed by Norma. But Caroline was looking down at her feet when Norma screamed.

Caroline jerked and stumbled against Ben. He reached out to steady her and she felt his solid chest against her shoulder blades for several long moments. Sarah shrieked and hopped to the side as a black raccoon with a striped tail ran beneath their feet and darted through the open doorway. The animal made a little chittering sound as it scurried down the steps, raced across the graveled driveway and disappeared into the bishop's hayfield.

"*Ach!* What was that?" Sarah asked, breathing hard.

"I have no idea but that animal scared me half to death." Norma pressed a hand to her chest as she took several deep inhales.

The other women appeared startled, too, glancing around for more intruders.

Caroline gasped. "Oh, *ne! Guck emol datt!* I can't believe it."

In unison, they turned to look at the schoolroom. Caroline's mouth dropped open and she gripped the handles of her crutches hard. The place was an absolute mess. Chewed-up bits of wood, paper and pencils were strewn across the wooden floor along with animal excrement. Dirty paw marks covered the tan walls and window casings. The blinds had been torn off the windows. Several of the desks were scratched up and one of the wooden legs had even been gnawed off. From across the room, Caroline noticed the curtain that covered the supply closet was ripped to shreds, as if the animal had used it to climb up to the top shelves.

As one body, they stepped inside and Ben held out a protective hand to the women. "Wait here a few minutes while I check to see if there are any more animals inside. Coons can be pretty fierce, especially if they feel cornered, and I don't want any of you to get hurt."

Grateful for his offer, Caroline watched silently as he searched every corner of the room, under her desk and inside the supply closet. Finally, he returned, a deep frown curving his full lips downward.

"It seems there was only one raccoon today, but I can tell there have been more in here. They've raised babies inside the supply closet this summer. I found their nest," he said with a deep sigh.

"But how did they get in?" Caroline asked.

"Come with me."

They all followed as he walked over to the supply closet and pointed up at the ceiling. Crowding close, they tilted their heads to get a better look. A hole just large enough for a raccoon to squeeze through had been gnawed through the air vent above, with more dirty paw tracks covering the walls.

"I had no idea they could chew through such things or that they could climb walls so well," Caroline said.

"*Ja*, they have sharp teeth and little arms and claws that work just like hands. It makes them very nimble," Ben said.

"Do you think they came through the crawl space in the rafters?" Caroline asked.

He nodded. "And once they got inside, they had free rein to do whatever they liked with the place."

"But how did they get into the crawl space?" Caroline asked, trying to understand so she could do something to stop it from happening again.

"I suspect we'll find that answer outside." He headed toward the door and Caroline followed.

Ben was tall and strong and moved pretty fast. It wasn't easy for her to walk, but as the teacher, she felt it was important for her to know exactly what was going on with her school. When he realized she was following him, Ben slowed down, patiently giving her time to catch up.

"*Ach*, I guess we've got a bigger cleanup job than I thought. While you two check out how the little bandits got inside, we're gonna get to work tidying up this mess," Becca called after them.

She hurried to take the bucket of cleaning supplies from Caroline, and the other women rolled up their sleeves in preparation of a long, hard day of work.

As Caroline made her way toward the door, she was beyond grateful they were all here. If she had faced this situation alone, she honestly didn't know what she would have done. Mentally, she was prepared to do whatever was necessary to make this teaching assignment work. But physically, she didn't have the strength or dexterity to do the chores by herself. Not yet, anyway.

Ben paused at the threshold, waiting for her. She still felt annoyed by his presence but was glad he was here right now. No doubt they would need some repairs to the ceiling, and she had no idea how she could climb up on a ladder without his aid. Maybe the bishop had been wise to assign Ben to help her after all.

Outside, they slowly made their way around the building. They perused the log sides for any holes and looked up at the roof for any openings that would give the animals access to the interior of the school.

"There it is!" Ben pointed up.

Caroline lifted her head and saw a piece of metal flashing that had been ripped away from the side of the rain gutter. She stared, feeling stunned by the ingenuity of the raccoons.

"But how can such a little creature climb up there

and pull all that metal away from the building?" she asked.

"Remember they have sharp claws and teeth. They're persistent little buggers." He chuckled, placing his hands on his hips and shaking his head.

He looked strong and masculine, and Caroline forced herself to look away. On the surface, Ben would make an ideal Amish husband. Devout, hardworking and kind. But what she knew about his past made it impossible for her to like him.

"The school board told me we had enough paper and other supplies for the school year, but it's all been destroyed by the raccoons. It looks like I'll need to make another trip into town to buy some more," Caroline said.

Ben nodded. "I'll drive you there once we're finished with the cleanup. I can drop you off at the general store while I go to the feed and grain supply to get a live animal cage trap."

She glanced at him. "You're going to trap the animal if it comes back?"

He nodded. "The live trap is a humane way of catching the raccoon, and then I'll take it into the mountains and release it far away from the school so it won't return and do more harm."

She knew many of her Amish people would just get a pellet gun and kill the little varmint. She liked that Ben was trying to preserve the raccoon's life. Although the animal had created quite a mess, she didn't wish it any harm. But she also didn't want it to come back. And neither did she like the idea of traveling all the way into town alone with Ben.

"I… I can drive myself and pick up the cage, too.

I'm sure the store owner will show me how to work the trap," she said.

Her words were false bravado and she knew it. Where wild raccoons were concerned, she was in way over her head. And what if Rand Henbury came upon her along the road?

Ben was shaking his head even before she could finish speaking. "*Ne*, I'll drive you there. I'll need to pick up some flashing, roofing supplies and nails, too, so I can repair the damage before bad weather sets in."

Yes, he was right. She definitely needed his help and didn't have the heart to argue with him right now.

He turned abruptly, cutting off any further reply, and waited for her to precede him back into the schoolhouse. As she lifted her elbow crutches and shuffled forward, she hated the thought of him walking behind her. She could feel him watching her, his eyes boring a hole in her back. The crutches were cumbersome and she was highly aware of how awkward and clumsy she must look. It made her even more determined to get rid of the crutches just as soon as possible. She couldn't stand the things!

With the other women's help, the floors were soon swept and mopped, the walls washed, the potbellied stove cleared of ashes, and the outhouse cleaned and readied for use. Ben tidied up the little horse barn and chopped more firewood in preparation for the colder mornings. They all worked cheerfully together, discussing the news of each *familye* in their *Gmay* and laughing often. Their happy chatter eased some of Caroline's tension and made her feel like she wasn't alone.

"Many hands make light work," Aunt Hannah commented as they stood back and perused their finished efforts.

"*Ja*, and now I've got to get home and prepare supper for my *familye*. Amos will be coming in from the fields soon," Sarah said.

Norma nodded in agreement. "Me, too."

Sarah looked at Hannah. "Ben has told me that he's going to drive Caroline into town in our buggy. Would you mind giving me a ride home on your way?"

"Of course not. Let's go," Hannah said.

Caroline stared at the women, wondering how to argue the point without sounding childish. After all, they all knew by now that the bishop had assigned Ben to work with her. In the end, she shut her mouth and accepted that he would be driving her into town and taking her home afterward.

They all stepped out into the afternoon sunshine. A dry, hot wind ruffled the ties on the women's white prayer *kapps*. They each rolled the long sleeves to their plain Amish dresses down to their wrists. Soon, the weather would change, and Caroline dreaded the ice and snow. From past experience, she knew it would make every surface slick and treacherous. She vowed right then and there that she would be walking without the aid of crutches before the first snowfall. The sooner she could walk on her own, the sooner she could get rid of Ben Yoder.

While she locked the front door, the others waved and said their farewells. She turned and found Ben standing beside the bishop's black buggy, waiting for her to join him. As she stepped forward, he hurried to assist her. Without asking permission, he reached out and took hold of her arm, his hand gentle but firm against her skin. And once more, she wished she could walk without any help.

The rhythmic *clip-clop* of the horse's hooves striking the black asphalt helped soothe Ben's jangled nerves as he drove Caroline into town. She sat as far away from him on the other side of the bench seat as possible. Her slender spine was rigid and she stared straight ahead, as if he weren't even there.

"I still don't understand why you have to drive me into town. I'm not incapable, you know. I don't need to walk well in order to drive myself. I just need to be able to sit." She spoke so suddenly that he flinched. Her voice sounded tense and thick with resentment, and he couldn't really blame her.

"I know you're capable of driving yourself, but I have my orders," he said.

She whirled around and stared at him hard, her eyes narrowed. "*Ja*, my *onkel* Mervin and Bishop Yoder put you up to this. I know all about it."

He nodded, unwilling to deny it. After all, he hadn't asked for this task. But neither would he shirk his duty.

"The bishop has given me the explicit assignment of helping you with all the needs of the school. I'm to look out for your welfare in all things, including repairing damage caused by the raccoons. I have to go into town to get supplies to do that, so it makes sense that we ride together. I promise to get you *heemet* safe and sound," he said.

There. That was good. Perhaps she wouldn't fight

him so hard if he reminded her that he was on orders from the bishop and the school board.

"*Ach*, so you're my bodyguard now?" she asked, her voice filled with incredulity.

"*Ne*, I'm just your assistant."

She gave a giant huff of indignation and faced forward again. He could tell from the stiff set of her shoulders and her tight expression that she wasn't happy about this. Not at all.

"I don't need a babysitter," she grumbled.

"I'm not your babysitter. I'm just here to work. I earned my school certificate and can do a lot to keep the kids in line during recess. I'm also very *gut* at reaching things on the top shelf." He suggested these ways he could be useful, wanting to soothe her tattered feelings. He didn't want her for an enemy.

She glanced at him and then a slight smile curved her lips, as if she couldn't stay angry at him any longer. "Hmm. So you're my teacher's assistant, huh? Do you always look for the good in things?"

Her smile lit up her face and made her eyes sparkle like blue cornflowers. He was utterly charmed and couldn't help returning her smile.

"*Ja*, I try to make the best of life. Sometimes it's not easy but I'd rather be happy than angry and sad," he quipped.

She frowned suddenly, as if remembering she didn't want to be friends with him.

"*Ach*, either way, it sounds like I'm your pet project now. No doubt the bishop is playing matchmaker again. He's done things like this before. Many times, in fact. Getting single people together so they'll fall in love and marry. But I should warn you right up front, I'm not interested," she said.

Wow! She sure was blunt. And he couldn't blame her. Why would a sweet young woman like Caroline Schwartz want anything to do with a big, gruff man like him? He was a killer. He wasn't in her league. She should find and marry any man but him.

It appeared the bishop's matchmaking efforts would be in vain.

"I understand. But the bishop didn't tell me he wanted me to court you. He just asked me to help you out with the school and keep you safe at all times," he said.

"Of course he wouldn't tell you that, but I've known your *onkel* for years now. As the bishop, he's eager to build our Amish community. And he does that by getting eligible couples together. He's said so in church on many occasions. No doubt he's hoping you and I will get together, too." She sounded rather grouchy and annoyed.

"*Onkel* Amos would never make us do anything we didn't want," he said. "Let's just make the best of the situation and think of the children we're serving, okay? I can assist you while you continue to heal, and I promise not to expect anything more. Once you're able to walk well enough on your own, I'll ask the bishop if I can stop coming to the school every day. Agreed?"

She peered at him suspiciously, as if she didn't believe him. He knew there was no way she could fight against the bishop and the other school board members. Not when it meant they could fire her from this job. But he'd rather not be the target of her resentment, either.

Finally, she nodded and raised her chin slightly

higher. "Agreed. For the time being. But I don't have to like it."

Whew! He was beyond relieved. He didn't want to do anything to upset the bishop or Sarah and their *familye*. Right now Ben was just grateful to have a place to live. A place that included his relatives and people of his own faith. Even if members of the *Gmay* still looked at him with suspicion and doubt, it was better than living in the *Englisch* world where he had no one at all. But neither did Ben want to upset Caroline. Whether she admitted it or not, she truly did need his help at the school. But it'd be a long, miserable winter if she kept fighting him on this. He'd rather they got along.

He parked the buggy in front of the general store and helped Caroline down. Although it was almost suppertime, the summer days were longer and the sun was still high in the sky. Thinking only of her safety, Ben was determined to get her home before dark.

As he escorted her to the front door, she struggled with her elbow crutches. He reached out to help, but she jerked away and he let her do it on her own. Her cute button nose was elevated slightly, showing her spunk. She was trying so hard, and he couldn't help appreciating her persistence.

"Will you be all right if I leave you for a few minutes? I need to go to the feed and grain store now," he said.

"Of course. I can do my own shopping." Her voice sounded rather tart, and he admired her flashing eyes for just a moment.

"*Gut.* And will you also buy a couple cans of cat food?" he asked.

Leaning forward on her crutches, she tilted her head in confusion. "What on earth for?"

"Raccoons love cat food. I'll use it as bait so I can trap them in the cage before relocating them far away from the school," he said.

"Ah, I see. *Ja*, I'll buy some cat food."

She turned and shuffled away. When he knew she was safely inside, he got in the buggy and drove down the street. And for the first time in a long time, he felt joyful inside. They had an agreement between them. A truce of sorts. It was a good plan that should make everyone happy, including the bishop and the school board. Ben would assist Caroline in any way possible and try to stay out of her way in the process. As soon as she was able to function well enough on her own, he would leave her alone and never bother her again.

It was what they both wanted. Wasn't it? So why did the thought of not being near her anymore make him feel so sad and empty inside?

Chapter Three

The following Saturday, Uncle Mervin drove Caroline to the schoolhouse early in the morning. It was customary to hold an all-school singalong and picnic before the start of school. All the students' families would be attending, including the school board members. For such an important event, she wanted to ensure everything was in order before the parents started arriving.

Brilliant sunlight gleamed against the shiny new flashings Ben had hung along the edge of the roof to repair the damage caused by the raccoons. As Mervin helped her out of the buggy and reached for her elbow crutches, Caroline hoped the varmints stayed away permanently. Maybe Ben had already caught one of the animals in his live cage trap. She shuddered at the thought of handling the coons on her own and was grateful he was dealing with the problem for her.

"I'll be back in time for the picnic in a couple of hours. Are you sure you'll be *allrecht* by yourself until then?" Mervin asked.

Caroline hesitated. A brief moment of panic flashed

through her mind. What if she fell down and couldn't get up? What if there was an emergency and she couldn't walk fast enough to get help?

Gathering her courage, she forced herself to show a bright smile. She must be positive. She must have faith!

"*Ja*, I'll be fine," she said.

With a nod, Mervin hopped back into the carriage and pulled away, leaving Caroline alone. As she watched the buggy fade from view, she took a deep breath and turned to face the schoolhouse. Walking toward it on her elbow crutches, she was startled to hear a tap-tapping sound coming from the side of the building. Now what?

Using caution, she rounded the log house, surprised to see Ben standing outside beneath the window nearest her teacher's desk. Holding a hammer, he pounded nails into a little white box he'd affixed just beneath the windowsill. She recognized it as a flower box.

"*Hallo*, Ben," she called without enthusiasm.

He jerked, startled, and hit his thumb with the hammer. She cringed, knowing it must have hurt.

"*Ach!*" he cried, dropping the tool to the ground. He turned to look at her and shook his hand, as if to ease the pain.

"Oh, I'm terribly sorry, Ben. I didn't mean to surprise you. Are you okay?" Realizing she'd distracted him, she hurried toward him as fast as she could move on the crutches.

Seeing her, he nodded and gave a half smile. "*Ja*, I'm fine. Nothing that won't heal in time."

Standing beside him, she looked up at his tall frame. She was completely alone with him and wasn't sure she liked that at all. They had a treaty between them, but she still felt uncomfortable in his presence.

"Why are you here so early?" she asked.

He squinted at the bright sunlight and his eyes crinkled. "I was going to ask you the same question."

She gestured toward the building. "I wanted to ensure everything was in order before the families start arriving. I also wanted to make sure no more raccoons have gotten inside the schoolroom."

He nodded, turning back to his work. "I've already checked inside and everything is in order. There are no raccoons in the trap I set up outside, either."

So. He had a key to the schoolhouse. Caroline knew without asking that the bishop must have given it to him.

She breathed a heavy sigh, grateful the raccoons were gone but feeling grumpy that Ben had a key to her inner sanctum. "*Gut.* I want everything nice and in order for the parents to see. I'd be mortified if they saw the classroom looking the way it did when we found it after the raccoons had been in there."

He chuckled. "I can't blame you for that."

He lifted his hammer and put some finishing touches on the flower box. It was pristine white, and she could see several more of the little boxes sitting nearby on the ground. Just enough for each window of the schoolhouse.

"What are you doing?" she asked.

Without meeting her gaze, he indicated the boxes. "Since you'll be cooped up inside teaching all day, I thought you might like to look out your window and see some pretty flowers during your workday. While you're occupied, you can look out the window anytime and hopefully, it will make you happy."

She stared, stunned by his consideration. Nearby on the ground were several bags of potting soil and flats of yellow and purple pansies. No doubt he intended to plant them inside the flower boxes.

"Let me guess. The bishop put you up to this, too," she said.

He stared with a blank expression. "*Ne*, I thought it up all by myself. If you don't like the flower boxes, I can take them away."

A flush of embarrassment heated her cheeks. She hadn't meant to offend him and searched her brain for something kind to say. "*Ne*, I love them, actually. It was very thoughtful of you, Ben. *Danke*. But how did you pay for the materials?"

He tapped the box he'd just hung beneath her window with one hand. "Consider them a gift from me to the school. The boxes look like wood but they're made of cellular PVC, so they won't rot like wooden boxes would. Each one comes with a self-watering reservoir, so you only have to fill the pipe once per week and then it wicks out from beneath the soil to water the roots of the plants underneath. Don't worry about lifting a heavy watering can to fill the reservoir. I'll take care of that chore for you."

She didn't know what to say. Seeing the white box affixed beneath her window, she could just envision a bunch of colorful pansies growing inside and loved what he had done. His gesture warmed her heart, and she couldn't help wondering if there was more to this big, gruff man than she'd first thought.

"You've been very kind. I can tell you put a lot of thought into this project. No doubt you're a *gut* carpenter," she said.

That wasn't surprising. Many of the men in her Amish community worked with wood and made all the furniture in their own homes. She was glad that Ben had this same talent. If not for his dark past, he would make some woman a fine husband.

He nodded. "I wanted the boxes to be beautiful but not require you to work too hard to keep them nice. Winter is coming, so the flowers won't last long. But pansies are hardy in the cold weather, and you should have a couple of months to enjoy their color before a killing frost arrives in our valley. Next summer I can plant other flowers for you. I was trying to get the project done in time for the back-to-school picnic but I don't think I'll quite make it."

Wow! He'd even put some thought into which plants to put in the boxes, to provide the longest growth possible before the cold set in. Yes, there was definitely more to this man than she'd first realized.

"It's *allrecht*. I think the parents will notice and like what you're doing anyway. They're beautiful, Ben. *Danke* so much," she said.

His features softened and he showed a slight smile. "You're not just saying that? You really like them?"

She nodded. "I really like them. A lot."

And it was the truth. She'd been cooped up so much in her convalescence and hadn't been able to get outside to plant and work in the garden like she used to. Being able to see flowers growing outside her desk window and around the rest of the schoolhouse as she worked each day would be more than pleasant. It would be cathartic.

He finally faced her. "Even though we didn't have a raccoon in the cage trap this morning, the bait was gone."

"What does that mean?" she asked, frowning as she shifted her weight to ease the ache at the small of her back.

"It means something was able to get inside the trap and steal the food away without getting caught."

"*Ach!* You don't think the animals will come back and destroy the classroom again, do you?" Caroline scanned the schoolyard, looking for any signs of the varmints. Right now her greatest desire was to keep things running smoothly so the school board realized she could do this job and do it well.

"Don't worry," he reassured her. "I've moved the cat food deeper inside the cage so the critters can't bypass the metal plate that closes the door. We'll catch one next time."

He sounded so sure of himself. So confident. And Caroline couldn't help feeling relieved. Right now she needed to focus on the students and lesson plans, not a pack of raccoons who could destroy the school.

"*Ach*, I better get inside now. The bishop should be coming soon with the tables to set up for the picnic." She gestured toward the red log building.

"I've already set up the tables and chairs down by the creek. I figured it would be pretty and offer more shade down there."

Setting his hammer aside, Ben took her arm without asking permission and led her toward the trees. The trickle of crystal-clear water met her ears. Sitting beneath the shade of several elm trees were a number of long tables and backless wooden benches—the same ones they used during their church services. The slight breeze rustled the leaves overhead and carried the light fragrance of honeysuckle. The spot was ideal for a picnic. So pleasant and lovely.

"My *aent* Sarah will be here soon with some plastic tablecloths to cover the tables for you," he said.

She blinked, beyond relieved by what he'd done. She had thought she would have to set the tables up by herself and wondered how she would manage. But she shouldn't be surprised. Her people were hard workers and took care of one another. She should have known they'd help her set this up, too. But more than that, she was finally starting to understand that Ben truly was going to be her constant companion for the time being.

"Wow! You're a good teacher's assistant. You've gone above and beyond the call of duty today. I appreciate it so much," she said.

He flashed a smile that lit up his brooding eyes and made her stare at his handsome face.

"You're *willkomm*," he said.

He turned and walked back to the flower boxes, continuing with his chore of hanging them beneath each window. Caroline watched him for a few moments, her mind churning. It seemed he'd truly taken to heart his assignment to look after the school. He was a dedicated and hardworking man. But she must never forget he had a foul temper and had killed another human being. That alone put up a wall between them that must never come down.

* * *

"*Komm* play with us, Ben!"

He turned and saw little Rachel Geingerich, Elijah Albrecht, Sam King and Andy Yoder gazing at him with hopeful expressions. He was surprised by their request, until he remembered they were no more than seven years old. Too young to know or care what he had done in his past.

Elijah held a red ball, which looked almost bigger than the child. Ben doubted they could bounce it well on the graveled playground, but they could sure play a game of keep-away.

Abandoning the flower boxes he'd been working on, he reached for Rachel and lifted her high in his arms. She squealed with delight, resting her small hands on his shoulders. The girl was so trusting, and he wished Caroline could feel the same way toward him.

"You want to play, do you?" He spoke to them in a teasing voice filled with the promise of fun.

"*Ja*, we do!" the boys called.

"*Allrecht!* Let's play keep-away. It'll be Rachel and me on one team and you boys on the other," he said.

The kids laughed and spread out in preparation for the game. Ben glanced over at the gathering of parents as they milled around the tables of food. Some of the adults were watching him with skeptical expressions. He ignored them, his gaze automatically seeking out Caroline. It had become a habit for him to watch over her, see what she was doing, anticipate her needs and help her out if he thought it was warranted. She always looked a bit irritated by him doing this.

Most of the parents and other children were congregated around the long tables he'd set up down by the creek. An hour earlier Caroline had led the children in several songs they'd learned last school year, and the crowd had then enjoyed the picnic lunches each *familye* had brought to share. As far as Ben was concerned, the day had been a great success. Caroline must be pleased.

He saw her standing beneath an elm tree, speaking with several parents. He could tell from the scrunch of her shoulders and the way she constantly shifted her feet to redistribute her weight on her legs that she was tired and needed to sit down. No one else seemed to notice, but he'd become highly tuned in to her body language.

"We'll play, but first, I need to take care of one tiny thing," he told the kids, holding up a finger.

"Ah!" The children groaned in dismay.

Setting Rachel down, he hurried over to retrieve a folding chair and placed it beside Caroline. She blinked at him in surprise. The parents she'd been chatting with also looked surprised but he paid them no mind.

"You should sit down and rest for a while," he said quietly.

As usual, her lips pinched together but he turned away before she could scold him. He saw a flash of disapproval in her eyes and knew she wasn't pleased by his interruption. Her gaze mirrored that of the other adults standing nearby. They didn't approve of him, either. But his gesture awakened their common courtesy.

"*Ach*, of course you should sit, Caroline. I'm sorry I didn't think of it myself." Linda Hostetler reached to take Caroline's crutches.

Satisfied that he'd tended to Caroline's needs, Ben returned to the children. They clapped their hands and jumped up and down with excitement. In their sweet faces, he saw nothing but trust and anticipation. And before he knew what was happening, they were chasing him around the playground. When he let them catch him, they mobbed him, laughing, climbing all over him and having a great time.

Their fun drew the attention of some of the adults. Looking up, Ben saw a few frown and shake their heads before whispering together behind their hands. No doubt they were discussing him and whether he was a good influence on their young children. But he didn't care. Not today. Because the kids were the only ones who didn't judge him. They took him at face value. When he was with them, he didn't have to worry about what they knew about his past. He didn't feel inadequate, either. He just had fun.

The afternoon passed quickly, and it was soon time to clean up and go home. Ben had installed three of the six flower boxes. Next week he would finish the project. But as he helped the other men load the benches and folding tables into the horse-drawn buggy-wagon to put them away, his gaze sought out Caroline once more. She was carrying a wicker basket filled with extra paper plates and plastic utensils over to her uncle's buggy and didn't pay him any mind. He leaned an arm against the wagon, wishing she would notice him and look his way—wishing just once that she would trust him as freely as the young children did. He longed to see her look at him without fear and repulsion in her eyes.

But he realized that hope would probably never come to fruition. He and Caroline would never marry, as the bishop had hoped. They might not even become friends. And that thought made him feel even worse.

Chapter Four

Caroline slid her McGuffey Reader into her school-bag, then reached for her red personal-size cooler that contained her lunch. Standing beside the kitchen sink in her uncle's home, she leaned her hip against the counter before opening the cooler and peering inside to see what Aunt Hannah had prepared for her: a ham sandwich and a wedge of *snitz* pie. Very nice.

"Where's Levi? He hasn't had his breakfast yet." Balancing her baby daughter on her hip, Aunt Hannah turned from the stove and scooped a wedge of scrapple onto the boy's plate before setting it on the table. Scrapple was like a wedge of meatloaf and was made of sausage, diced apple, sage and cornmeal. Very filling and delicious.

The other children crowded around the long table. The loud sounds of their conversations and the clatter of eating utensils permeated the room. Mervin had gone out to the barn over an hour earlier and would soon be coming inside for his own meal.

"I'll get him." Little five-year-old Benuel slid off his

chair and ran to the foot of the stairs before hollering up. "Levi! *Komm* and eat."

"Benuel, stop yelling. Go to your brother's room to get him!" Aunt Hannah called in an equally loud voice.

Caroline cringed at the noisy racket. Though she was used to the daily chaos in this home, she was beyond distracted with her own thoughts today. Forcing herself to concentrate, she reached into the gas-powered fridge for an orange and a bag of raw carrots to round out her lunch. After placing them inside the cooler, she snapped the lid closed, then swiveled on her crutches and took a deep inhale. It was the first day of school and she was ready to go. Maybe she should return to her room, just to be alone and gather her thoughts for a few minutes.

The rattle of a horse and buggy coming from outside drew her attention and she glanced at the clock on the wall. Her uncle Mervin was early this morning. Surely, he wouldn't take her to school before eating his breakfast. Or maybe the driver was Alice, Caroline's fourteen-year-old cousin, who would accompany her to school along with her three younger siblings.

After hobbling over to the window, Caroline moved aside the plain brown curtains and peered outside. The sun had just peeked over the eastern mountains, spraying the sky with highlights of pink and gold. Chickens scratched in the yard and she caught the contented lowing of the milk cows out in the pasture.

A black buggy was parked in the backyard but the driver was nowhere to be seen. Caroline didn't recognize the roan horse and realized it wasn't her uncle after all. Who could be visiting the farm so early on a Monday morning?

A knock on the back door caused her to turn.

"I'll get it." Benuel raced past the long table and chairs and gripped the knob with both hands as he tugged open the door.

Ben Yoder's wide shoulders filled the threshold. Dressed in his everyday work clothes, his straw hat shaded his expressive eyes.

"Ben! *Komm* in. Have you had your breakfast?" Aunt Hannah asked. She held a plate of sizzling sausages, hot off the stove.

He stepped into the room, his gaze resting on Caroline.

"*Ja*, I've eaten. I've *komm* to drive Caroline to school," he said, his voice low and matter-of-fact.

Caroline stared at him, shocked to her toes. "But… but I didn't ask you to do that. Alice is going to drive me."

"*Ne*, she'll drive the other *kinder* later on, after they've finished their morning chores," Aunt Hannah said. "Since you need to go so early and *komm* home later in the afternoon, Ben is here to drive you now. Alice will need to *komm* home right after school so she and the other *kinder* can finish their evening chores before supper. Ben will drive you home once you're finished with your work. He'll stay at the school until you're ready to leave."

Confusion fogged Caroline's brain. She hadn't expected this at all.

"But that wasn't the agreement. Ben is only helping me out at school. Right?" She couldn't believe this. Surely Ben Yoder wasn't going to be her constant companion every waking moment. Or was he?

"Until you're able to drive yourself, the bishop asked that I accompany you to and from school, as well. He doesn't want you out on the roads alone in case Rand Henbury should come upon you and spook your horse." Ben spoke in a quiet voice, as if sensing her discomposure.

Oh, no! This just kept getting worse.

"But he didn't tell me that. I thought you were just going to be hanging around the schoolyard, not coming into my home and driving me around all the time." A flush of heat suffused Caroline's face. Only now did she realize just how far the bishop's orders extended. But she hadn't planned on this. It was too much for her to accept.

"It's what the school board wants," Aunt Hannah said, as if that settled everything.

Great! Even Aunt Hannah was in on this. Dawning flooded Caroline's brain. Ben had truly been assigned to be her constant companion. He would stay with her throughout the day, morning to evening. Always there. Watching over her. Waiting upon her. Seeing to her every need. A relentless shadow.

A huge nuisance.

"But I don't need a chaperone on my way to school. Surely, you have better things to do with your day," she said, unable to keep a note of exasperation from her voice.

"I have plenty of other work that could occupy me, but the bishop and his sons have taken over those chores. He believes the work I will do with you is imperative right now. I agree with him that your well-being is of paramount importance," he said.

She was conscious of his silent gaze resting on her like a ten-ton sledge. And then it occurred to her. Maybe he didn't want to be with her, either. After all, what fun could it be to accompany a woman around all day long? Helping her in and out of the buggy. Holding her arm while she negotiated the stairs. Repairing messes made by the raccoons. Maybe this wasn't easy for him, either.

Aunt Hannah lifted Caroline's lunch box off the counter and handed it to Ben. She did have the good grace to look a bit sheepish, telling Caroline that she had known about this all along and had neglected to inform her about it.

"Of course you don't need a chaperone, dear," Aunt Hannah said. "You're quite capable. But right now Ben is your driver. And while you're at school, think of him as your handyman. I know a lot of previous teachers who would have loved to have a full-time assistant helping them out."

Like who? Becca Graber sure hadn't needed a full-time assistant last year. Caroline knew of no one who would have been happy with this arrangement. She stared at her lunch box as it swung easily from Ben's long fingertips. He stepped aside to give her access to the door, but she couldn't move. Couldn't breathe. It felt as if her feet were stapled to the floor.

"Are you ready?" he asked in that deep, calm voice of his.

She flinched. Unable to find an excuse to delay their departure, she nodded and scooted her elbow crutches forward before taking several steps. What choice did she have? It was either accept Ben's constant presence or face the bishop and school board. Neither option thrilled her.

At the threshold, he gripped her arm with his free hand and helped her over the bumps of the back porch and down the steps. She longed to throw him off. To snap at him to leave her alone. But that would mean giving in to the foul temper she'd accused him of having. She would sound like an old harpy and a hypocrite. And besides, she really did need his help.

For now.

Instead, she accepted his assistance as he helped her climb into the buggy. Then he hurried around to the driver's seat.

Once she was settled in, he took up the lead lines and slapped them gently against the horse's back. The buggy lurched forward and they were off. What followed was a long, awkward silence. They'd pulled onto the county road before either of them spoke again.

"Your *onkel* must need your help with chores on his farm," she finally said.

"*Ne*, I have been assigned to take care of you and the school. Until you no longer need me, that's what I intend to do."

So. Caroline really was Ben's full-time job, including buggy time. It wasn't as if there weren't enough hands at the bishop's farm to help with all the chores there. Bishop Yoder and Sarah had a large *familye* of very capable children. But still. Caroline hated to pull Ben away from his other work like this. It reminded her that she was impaired, and it made her even more determined to get rid of the crutches as soon as possible.

They rode in silence most of the way to the school.

When they arrived, she had to endure Ben's gentle touch as he helped her out of the buggy and escorted her up the front steps. When he swung the front door wide, she hesitated, dreading what she might find inside. If the raccoons had returned, she'd be forced to clean up the mess before she could begin teaching. But everything looked fine and she breathed a sigh of relief.

She hobbled over to her desk and set her bookbag on top. Looking out the window, she saw a spray of deep purple and yellow pansies in the window box Ben had installed there. They trembled in the mild breeze and looked lovely. A constant reminder of Ben's presence in her life.

"I'll get some drinking water and firewood." He picked up the clean water pitcher off the corner of her desk and turned toward the door.

"It's still hot outside. I doubt we'll need a fire today," she called.

He nodded. "Just in case."

She watched as he disappeared out the door. Through the window, she saw him pulling on the water pump to fill the pitcher, then he tucked several chunks of wood beneath his free arm. By the time he returned, she'd gathered her composure and stood in front of the chalkboard, writing out the day's lesson plans.

"We've caught a raccoon in the live cage trap." He set the pitcher of water on her desk with a little thud.

Caroline cringed, startled by this news. "*Ach*, he came back, then?"

"*Ja, she* has returned. But she won't cause you any trouble." Ben looped his thumbs through his black suspenders, looking rather solemn. "Some of the students have started arriving and will be coming inside now. If you're okay for the time being, I'll take the raccoon for a ride and release her several miles away from the school."

She caught his meaning. With students here, she wouldn't be alone and he could leave to take care of the chore. And even though he'd been more than kind, she couldn't help feeling like a little child who needed constant supervision. His mere presence raised the hairs on the back of her neck, and she couldn't help bristling.

"You can do whatever you like, Ben Yoder. It doesn't matter one single bit to me," she said.

He paused, his dark eyes unblinking. Then he tugged on the brim of his straw hat and spoke most gently. "As you wish. When I return I'll be putting together some of the new playground equipment. You'll be teaching school by then. If you need me for anything at all, just send one of the kids outside to get me."

Before she could respond, he turned and walked away, his long arms moving rhythmically with his stride. She stared after him, stunned and feeling a bit unworthy. In spite of her tart words, he'd offered no biting comments or angry facial expressions. Instead, he'd extended a kind invitation.

As she watched him go, it occurred to her that she may have hurt his feelings. That she was being ungrateful and unkind. And yet, she felt as if he'd been foisted upon her. An unwanted burden she wished would go away.

His offer to help reminded her that he was here to stay. Short of mutiny and openly defying the school board, there was nothing she could do to get rid of Ben.

Though she felt mightily uncomfortable around this man, she should at least try to get along and be polite. But she sure didn't have to like it.

She was watching him. Ben could feel Caroline's gaze drilling a hole in his back. Crouching over the new swing set he was putting together, he resisted the urge to turn and look up. But he knew she was there, sitting at her desk, gazing at him from the window in her classroom, watching him work.

He'd just returned from taking the raccoon and re-leasing it several miles away. The weather was still warm, so the animal should be able to find a new home without any trouble. He hoped they'd have no more var-mints in the school but had reset the cage trap just in case there was more than one.

Now he was tightening a bolt on the new swing set he was putting together. When he finished, he stood straight to ease a cramp in his lower back. As he reached for another screw, he couldn't resist glancing at the schoolhouse. Sure enough, Caroline sat primly at her desk, gazing out her window at him. When she caught his eye, she jerked and looked away, as if embarrassed to be caught staring.

The white flower boxes with the purple and gold pansies offered a pretty frame for her, and he watched her for several moments. She wore a black dress with a white cape and apron. The colors suited her but made her delicate skin seem that much paler. But what he wasn't prepared for was the startled look on her face. She didn't want him here. She'd made that clear. But more than that, he thought she hated him. He'd been thrust upon her by the school board, and she could hardly abide his presence.

She ducked her head over her paperwork, her pencil moving fast as she jotted some notes. He could just imagine the pink stain of discomfiture on her cheeks.

Acting casual, he turned back to his task and tried to gather his own thoughts. At the end of the previous school year, they'd held a boxed social fund-raiser to earn enough money to pay for a variety of playground equipment. It was now Ben's job to put it all together. Over the next few days he'd dig holes and sink the stands of the swing set, teeter-totter and tether ball into cement so they wouldn't tip over on the kids. He enjoyed the work. It occupied his time while he waited for the school day to end. When Caroline was ready, he would drive her home. And right now he dreaded the long ride. Mostly because he knew it would be filled with resentful silence. But more than anything, he wished he could make her smile instead.

Kneeling on the ground, he kept working and had the frame of the swing set put together by the time Caroline rang the noon bell. In a burst of energy, the front door was thrown open and the children poured forth into the schoolyard, carrying their variety of lunch buckets with them. They all scurried his way, mostly to see what he was doing. The older children hung back, watching him with quiet curiosity. The younger children crowded closer.

"What are you doing?" six-year-old Elijah Albrecht asked, winding his free hand around his black suspenders.

"What does it look like I'm doing?" Ben returned in

a pleasant voice as he reached for a Phillips screwdriver from his silver toolbox.

"Like you're building a swing set," Elijah said.

Ben chuckled and reached up to ruffle the boy's unruly hair. "*Ja*, that's exactly what I'm doing. You're a smart boy."

"Swing sets are for girls," Enos Albrecht said, scowling with disgust.

Ben continued to tighten another bolt as he spoke. "*Ach*, boys can enjoy a swing set just as well as girls."

"Not me. I wouldn't be caught dead on a swing," Caleb said. He was Ben's twelve-year-old cousin and a tad precocious.

"Why don't you build us a backstop for our baseball diamond instead?" one of the older boys asked.

Ben looked up, smiled and winked. "That's a *gut* idea. Maybe I will, in time. But you should always put your *weibsleit* first. And right now I'm building them a swing set."

Ben spoke from his heart. His uncles had taught him to put the womenfolk first. If he had a wife, he would treat her like a queen. And he realized he probably felt that way because a woman of his own was something he dearly wanted but would never have, so he appreciated the sentiment even more.

Enos tilted his head in confusion. "But you just said the swings were for the girls and the boys."

Ben nodded, trying not to chuckle. "*Ach*, they're mostly for the girls, though."

"Aha! I told you so," Enos exclaimed.

A deep laugh escaped Ben's throat. He couldn't help himself. "It's true, but I'm sure they'd be happy to share if you want to ride the swings, too. You can pretend you're flying."

"Not me!" Enos vowed.

"Or me, either," Caleb said.

Ben shook his head at the two children. "*Ach*, you boys have a lot to learn."

"Scholars! Leave Ben alone so he can do his work. Go on and eat your lunches now, then you can play for a while."

They all turned in unison and saw Caroline standing on the front steps to the school, holding a heavy desk bell in one hand. That wasn't an easy task since she was also trying to manage her elbow crutches at the same time. She leaned heavily on the crutches and Ben got the impression she was overly tired today. Not surprising, since it was the first day of school. She was spirited and determined, but he feared she was not as strong as she thought she was.

As the children raced over to the baseball diamond to gobble down their lunches before playing a quick game, Ben longed to ask Caroline if she was okay. Fearing her sharp response, he was slow to get the words out before she turned and shuffled back inside.

He worked for ten minutes more, then reached for his own lunch. Before he sat in the cool shade along Grape Creek to eat his food, he stepped over to the open doorway of the schoolhouse and peered inside. As usual, Caroline sat at her desk, grading papers. Her sandwich and an orange sat ignored beside her on the desk.

"Ahum!" He cleared his throat, not wanting to disturb her, yet he felt compelled to speak.

She lifted her head in weary acknowledgment. "*Ja*, Ben. What do you need?"

"Nothing at all, Caroline. I was just wondering if I could get you anything?" he returned.

"*Ne*, please just leave me alone."

He nodded without guile. "As you wish."

Turning, he walked outside. He didn't disturb her again until the last student had left the school at the end of the day. And still he kept working and waiting for some sign from her that she was ready to go home.

Finally, she stepped outside and turned to lock the front door. Without a word, he came to take her arm and helped her into the buggy. He could tell from the tilt of her head and the slump of her shoulders that she was too tired to object.

On the ride home, she was quiet as usual. He let her think, giving her the space she seemed to desire. When she finally spoke, he forced himself not to flinch in surprise.

"Did everything go *allrecht* with the raccoon this morning?" she asked.

He nodded, looking straight ahead. "*Ja*, the animal is fine."

"You…you didn't hurt it, did you?"

He caught the hesitancy in her voice and glanced her way.

"Of course not. I let her go, just as I said I would. The moment I lifted the cage door, she took off like a shot into the woods. I'm sure she'll be just fine."

She nodded, gazing at the trees and lush green fields flashing past the side of the road as the buggy hurried forward. "*Gut*. I wouldn't want the scholars to think we had killed the varmint, although I'm glad to have it gone."

He could understand her reasoning. He preferred not to have to clean up another mess, too. But some of the littler kids such as Rachel and Fannie were soft-hearted and might feel bad if they thought he'd hurt one of *Gott's* creatures needlessly.

"I reset the trap, just in case there are more," he said.

She whirled on him so fast that his gaze clashed then locked with hers. She pressed a hand to her chest and he gazed into her beautiful blue eyes, feeling helplessly lost there for several profound moments.

"You don't think there are more, do you?" she asked, an edge of urgency tainting her voice. No doubt she feared the school might get torn up again.

He smiled and turned away, trying to alleviate her qualms. "*Ne*, I think they're all gone now. But I want to make sure. I'll leave the trap where it is for the time being and check it each day. And I would suggest that someone check on the school regularly next summer when school is not in session. That way, the animals won't move in again. But don't worry about it. I'll take care of it if any more show up."

She exhaled a shallow sigh, her shoulders relaxing slightly as she rested her hands in her lap. "*Danke*, Ben. I'm grateful to you."

Ben's heart skipped a beat. Just a few simple words of gratitude, yet they meant everything to him. For the first time in years, he finally felt like someone really needed him. Not just for what he could do for them, but because they couldn't do it for themselves.

Even though Caroline didn't want him here, he

thought perhaps she was beginning to appreciate his talents just a teensy bit. And right now he didn't dare ask for anything more.

Chapter Five

Caroline awoke with a start. She stared at the ceiling in her bedroom for several moments. Thick darkness gathered around her, though an eerie red light flared in steady rhythm just outside her open window. A brief squawk of static broke the stillness of the night. It sounded like a radio but she couldn't be sure. She peered through the shadows at the clock on the wall. Just past three in the morning. What on earth was going on?

Flipping the covers back, she sat up and clasped the handles of her elbow crutches before shuffling over to the window. As she did so, she noticed her legs weren't as stiff as they had been a week earlier and knew she was gaining in strength every day.

Peering down below, she saw a police car parked outside in the farmyard. The red emergency light on top of the car went out suddenly, and an officer got out of the car. He was accompanied by an *Englisch* woman dressed in blue jeans and a dark sweater, two Amish men and two young Amish children. Through the darkness, Caroline couldn't make out any of their faces, but she recognized the wide set of shoulders on one of the Amish men.

Ben Yoder.

She barely had time to consider what he was doing here at this time of night. A loud, hollow knock sounded on the front door. It echoed through the entire building, and she feared it might wake up the whole household.

As she drew away from the window, Caroline heard her uncle and aunt's voices coming from their room across the hall.

"What is it? Who could be coming to our house in the middle of the night?" Aunt Hannah asked in a hushed whisper.

"I don't know. I'll go and check. You stay here where it's warm," Uncle Mervin replied.

His consideration of her aunt touched Caroline's heart. How she wished there was a man somewhere in this world who might love her the way Uncle Mervin loved her aunt.

Within moments the stairs creaked as he went down to see what was amiss. But it wasn't long before Aunt Hannah went downstairs, too.

Curiosity got the better of Caroline. Turning, she pulled on her modest robe and secured the belt tightly around her waist. With several quick movements, she twisted her long hair into a bun at the nape of her neck and pulled her white prayer *kapp* over top to hide the golden strands.

The scrape of a chair and low voices came from just below. The visitors must be in the main living room. She recognized Uncle Mervin's voice but didn't know the strangers. Except for Ben, who didn't speak.

It took her a little time before she could hobble to the door and step out on the landing. Slowly, she made her way downstairs. As she stepped into the living room, she blinked at the bright gas light filling the area. Her gaze immediately took in the sight of Aunt Hannah fully dressed and sitting in a chair at the end of the sofa, her face buried in her hands. Her shoulders trembled as she wept softly. Uncle Mervin stood behind her, one of his gruff hands resting on her arm in silent comfort.

As Caroline came near, she didn't speak, waiting for the problem to be revealed. The police officer stood beside the front door, his dark blue uniform, badge and holstered gun a glaring contrast to the humble Amish home he'd invaded. The *Englisch* woman stood facing the sofa, her silvery eyes filled with sad compassion as she held a manila file folder in her arms.

Sitting on the couch were Bishop Yoder and Ben. Two young Amish children dressed in traveling clothes sat huddled between them, their eyes wide, faces pale and tear-stained. Caroline guessed the girl looked to be about five and the boy around six. The boy held a tattered straw hat in his lap that was flattened beyond repair. Ben had lifted one arm up along the back of the couch and wrapped it around the two children's shoulders, his big hand dwarfing them both. And without asking, Caroline knew the kids must belong to their cousins from Ohio. Uncle Mervin was planning to pick up the *familye* from the bus station in town first thing in the morning. But where were their parents? Anna and James should be here, too. And why were Bishop Yoder and Ben here?

"What's happened?" Caroline finally asked, shuffling farther into the room.

"*Ach*, Caroline! They're gone. James and Anna. They've been killed." Aunt Hannah spoke in *Deitsch* as she popped out of her seat and ran to her and hugged her tight, sobbing against her shoulder.

"What?"

A sick feeling of shock and pain enveloped Caroline. It couldn't be true. Dear Anna. She was Caroline's first cousin once removed. Anna's mother and Caroline's grandmother had been sisters. And though they weren't related, Caroline had known James all her life. They'd grown up together in the same Amish community in Ohio. The couple couldn't be gone. They just couldn't.

She did her best to comfort her aunt while still keeping hold of her crutches. Over Aunt Hannah's head, she met Mervin's gaze and saw the forlorn look in his eyes.

"Anna and James…were killed this evening," Mervin confirmed.

Caroline gasped. She couldn't stop herself. A sharp pain speared her heart and a rush of tears filled her eyes.

"I'm afraid there was a bad accident on I-70, just outside of Denver," the officer said. "We believe the driver of a semi-truck fell asleep at the wheel. When he lost control, he crossed the median and drove into oncoming traffic. Four people died, including the driver and the children's parents."

Caroline's heart gave a powerful squeeze. She could hardly absorb what she was hearing. It was too much. Too horrific. She understood the ramifications only too well. It didn't matter whose fault it was. The two children sitting before her were now orphans.

"My name is Sharon Wedge. I'm a social worker with CPS." The *Englisch* woman looked all businesslike as she stepped forward and extended her hand.

As if in a fog, Caroline wiped her eyes and shook the woman's hand. "CPS? What is that?"

"Child Protective Services. Since both the children's parents were killed tonight, I was called in to help with their placement," Sharon said.

Placement? Like in a foster home?

"They brought the children to my house and I directed them here. I've explained that this was their final destination," Bishop Yoder said.

The policeman nodded. "That's right. The kids weren't exactly sure where they were supposed to go, but we knew Bishop Yoder would be able to help us figure it out since he's the leader of you Amish people living in the area."

Yes, this was true. There wasn't much that happened in the lives of the Amish people in Riverton that Bishop Yoder didn't know about.

Hearing this exchange, little Mary turned her face toward Ben and burrowed close against his side, her small hand clasping a fold of his blue shirt.

"There, there." Ben soothed her by patting her tiny arm with his free hand. Her muffled sobs sounded like a shout in the quiet room.

Watching Ben comfort the little girl did something to Caroline inside. She was crying, too, the tears running freely down her face.

"You should sit down, Caroline." Ben's gentle voice reached her as he inclined his head toward a hard-backed chair.

How dare he? Even in the middle of the night, when she was in her own home, he presumed to tell her what to do.

As if spurred into action, Mervin took her arm and led her to the chair. She sat for just a moment, her mind churning. She didn't want Mary and Seth to be placed in a foster home. She didn't want any of this. It wasn't right for them to lose their parents this way. It wasn't!

"Since you are their cousins and they were on their way to live here with you, I think we can let the children stay here for the time being," Sharon said.

Caroline shifted her weight, feeling nervous and upset. She'd heard horror stories of CPS getting involved in the lives of Amish children and didn't want to see Mary and Seth taken away and forced to live in an *Englisch* foster home.

"And what about the future? Mary and Seth are Amish. We are their family and I am their new schoolteacher. They should remain here with us," she said.

"That is true. We are their people." Bishop Yoder sat straighter, his expression stern.

Sharon smiled kindly. "I agree. Mr. Schwartz has given me some contact information and I'll make inquiries. But from what I've been told, you are the children's closest living relatives. I have no problem letting them stay here for now."

For now. But what about later on? Would CPS start meddling in the children's lives? Above all else, the Amish kept to themselves. They didn't want the *Englischers* to force their worldly ways upon them. Especially not on two young, impressionable children who had just lost their parents.

"We are their *familye*. They belong here with us," Uncle Mervin said.

Bravo! Caroline was pleased by her uncle's support.

Sharon didn't respond. She just looked at all the adults gathered in the room, seeming to assess each one of them in turn. On the one hand, Caroline was glad someone was looking out for them. But on the other, she didn't want this *Englisch* woman to start making decisions for these two Amish kids.

"I'm afraid the children's bags were lost in the accident," the police officer said. "It'll take some time to sort through the wreckage. We'll bring their luggage to you as soon as we can identify what is salvageable and what belongs to them."

Aunt Hannah didn't say a word. Her eyes were glazed and she stared with shock, so Caroline took charge.

"That's fine. We'll make sure they have everything they need in the meantime," she said.

The poor dears. The two kids looked frightened and exhausted. Right now they needed love and reassurance. And a good night's sleep, of course.

Caroline used one of her crutches to push herself up. As she stood, her gaze locked with Ben's. She saw something in his eyes, an emotion she didn't understand. Compassion, maybe? Or pity? She wasn't sure which. Maybe both.

She walked over to the children and extended one hand as she spoke in *Deitsch*. Amish children didn't learn to speak English until they started going to school at age five. These children were still young and might not know how to speak English very well, if at all. She would have knelt before them but couldn't manage that movement with her crutches.

"I'm your cousin Caroline," she said. "You probably don't remember me, but I remember you and your parents very well. I used to hold and feed both of you when you were very little *bopplin*."

Seth nodded and sat forward just a bit, seeming relieved to meet someone he could identify with. "*Ja, Mamm* told us about you. She said you used to pick apples with her in our orchard."

Caroline smiled. "That's right. We bottled apples and applesauce and made cider together. Are you hungry? Why don't we get you both a cup of hot cocoa and a slice of *schnitz* apple pie? Then we'll tuck you right into bed."

She held her breath, hoping no one objected. Hoping the two children came along willingly.

"That's a *gut* idea. *Komm* on." Ben slid forward and got to his feet.

Without asking permission, he leaned down and pulled little Mary into his arms. The girl promptly laid her head on his shoulder, looking at them all with huge round eyes and a pink rosebud mouth. Ben reached out and took Seth by the hand. The little boy followed eagerly, as if desperate to escape the room. They went into the kitchen, leaving Bishop Yoder, Uncle Mervin, Aunt Hannah, the policeman and social worker alone to work out the details. Ben sat in a hard-backed chair with Mary on his knee. Seth sat beside him, turned toward Ben as if he were a lifeline and the boy might need to latch on to him at any moment.

After all that had happened, it seemed strange for the kids to gravitate toward Ben, given that they'd just met the man. Perhaps it was his broad shoulders that drew them to him, which Caroline thought must seem strong and comfortable for a child to rest against.

Tomorrow was a regular school day, and they'd all be up early for morning chores. Maybe it was best to leave Mary and Seth home for the day. They needed time to recover in a quiet, loving home, without any other pressures on them. Caroline made a mental note to suggest this to Aunt Hannah just as soon as the *Englischers* left their home.

As Caroline went about dishing up pieces of pie, she listened to Ben's soft voice. He spoke to the kids about inconsequential things, though they didn't respond even once. But they clung to him, especially Mary. They seemed to trust him completely. And knowing about Ben's past, that surprised Caroline most of all.

Ben sat at the kitchen table with the children, one on each side of him. Mary stared at her hands in her lap while Seth leaned back and stared at the wall. It was as if they'd both pulled into themselves, ignoring the rest of the world. And Ben couldn't blame them. He'd done the same thing when he'd lost both his parents at a young age.

He watched as Caroline poured fresh milk into a pan and slid it onto the stove. While it heated, she sliced several pieces of *schnitz* apple pie. Her steady, purposeful movements seemed so calm and soothing in this atmosphere of gloom. She moved methodically, and he thought she did it so she wouldn't fall with her crutches. She seemed to have her routine down quite well. He felt the urge to get up and help her but thought the kids needed him more right now.

Caroline set the plates of pie on the table. He noticed she'd given him some, too. As the kids picked up their forks and took a bite, the room was absolutely quiet. Only the low sounds of voices coming from the living room and the bubbling of milk on the stove could be heard.

"Is that *gut*?" Ben smiled at the children, keeping his tone light and positive.

Mary nodded and cast a shy glance at him, but Seth didn't respond. The boy just stared steadfastly at his plate as he chewed. It was obvious they were hungry, for they wolfed down the pie. Ben had no idea when they'd eaten last and thought Caroline had been wise to offer them food. Especially something sugary and sweet. They needed it right now to help alleviate the shock they were undoubtedly feeling.

"Here we are. Some nice hot cocoa will warm you right up on the inside and help you feel better. Be careful not to burn your mouth." Caroline poured the frothy brown liquid into three mugs before sliding them closer to the children.

"*Danke*, Caroline." Ben picked up his mug, blew on the steaming mixture, then took a shallow sip. "Um, it's very tasty but definitely hot."

The two kids just stared at their cups, their eyes wide and glazed with moisture. Ben remembered that look from his own life. Disbelief. Shock. Grief.

No doubt the kids were wondering what had happened to their world. And though each of their situations were completely different, he couldn't help thinking they were all alike in a way. Ben and Caroline had both lost so much, and so had the kids. Though Seth and Mary still had each other, they were alone in the world, just like Ben and Caroline. Yes, they had their *Gmay*, their Amish people, and even relatives who cared about them. But they were still alone in so many ways. In his heart, he said a silent prayer asking *Gott* to be with them and provide comfort right now.

Caroline slid into the chair next to Mary and lifted a hand to caress the little girl's cheek. "Try some cocoa, my *liebchen*. It'll help you feel better so you can sleep."

As she held the cup for the girl, Mary took a shallow drink. When she pulled the cup away, the girl had a little mustache on her upper lip. She licked it off and lifted her brown eyes to gaze at Caroline.

"My *mammi* is gone for *gut*, isn't she?" Mary said, her voice filled with tears. In the quiet room, her words seemed like a shout. The statement was so final. So real.

"Our *daed* is gone, too," Seth said, his voice sounding thick with resentment.

Yes, these two kids were just like Ben and Caroline. The hurt. The anger and bitterness he'd felt all these years.

"*Ja*, they are gone, but you're not alone. We're here and you'll always have us," Ben said.

Caroline glanced at him and blinked. Maybe he'd spoken out of turn. Maybe he shouldn't give them false hope. And yet, he couldn't stand to have them go through life feeling isolated or like they had no one who really loved them.

"That's right," Caroline said, showing that soft and sincere smile of hers. "You have many people who love and care for you right here in this home. You're a part of our *familye*. You have us forever. You'll never be alone. Not ever."

Ben blinked, thinking she must have read his thoughts exactly.

Leaning heavily on her crutches, she stood and stepped away from the table. "*Ach*, I think it's time for you two to be in bed now. *Komm* with me, please."

Ben noticed that she'd used her kind but authoritative teacher voice. When she beckoned to them, the children didn't argue. They each scooted back their chairs, and Ben almost flinched when little Mary took his hand. As he accompanied them upstairs, something went all soft and mellow inside his chest.

Caroline stumbled on the stairs and Ben reached out to clasp her arm. As she found her balance, she nodded her thanks. Since Mervin and Hannah's children were already sleeping, they didn't turn on a light. In the dark, Ben helped Seth as he got ready for bed and slid beneath the covers next to one of his little cousins.

"I think it would be best to put the two *kinder* near each other tonight. Mary can sleep over here with Alice," Caroline whispered for his ears alone.

Ben nodded, once again impressed by her insight.

While he stood beside the open door, she sat with the kids for several minutes. Mary closed her eyes and slept almost instantly, but Seth rolled on his side and faced the wall. From the vague moonlight gleaming through the dark window, Ben could see the boy's eyes were open, his body tense. He was a bit older than Mary and not so quick to forgive what had happened to them tonight.

"I'll be right across the hall if you need me. *Gutte nacht*," Caroline whispered as she stood and shuffled to the door.

Ben took her arm to help her but she shook him off.

"I'm fine, *danke*. I don't need any help," she said.

He let her go, feeling stung by her dismissal. She pulled the door closed but left it slightly ajar, in case the children called out in the night.

"Do you think they'll be *allrecht*?" Ben asked as they stood together on the landing. He caught her fragrance, a clean, fresh smell that he quite liked.

"*Ja*, I'll look in on them later, before I go back to bed," she whispered.

She looked up at him and, for just a few moments, he gazed into her brilliant blue eyes. They stood there, locked in silence. There was so much he longed to confide in Caroline. So much he wanted to say. But he feared her disapproval too much.

"They're just like you and me. They're all alone in the world," he said, then instantly regretted it.

She might take his statement the wrong way. He didn't know why this woman was so easy to talk to. Maybe because of what they'd both lost, he thought they had a lot in common.

"*Ne*, they're not alone. Nor are you and I. We each have this *Gmay* and we have our Savior. He is always with us, no matter what trials we must face in this life. We are never alone, because we have Him," she said.

With those gentle words, she turned and worked her way downstairs. Her solid faith amazed him, and he wished he could discuss it with her a bit longer. But now wasn't the time.

No doubt she was eager to talk to her uncle and find out more details about the night's events. So was Ben. Above all else, he didn't want the *Englischers* to interfere and try to take Mary and Seth away from their Amish *familye*.

As he followed Caroline into the living room, he thought about what she'd said. They were never alone. Yet, in his darkest moments after his parents died, Ben had not felt the Lord near him. Of course, he hadn't been looking for *Gott*, either. Maybe if he had, he wouldn't have gone through life filled with so much anger and bitterness. And he hated the thought that Seth and Mary might do the same thing now that they were orphans.

Maybe he could make a difference in the two children's lives. And though Caroline had her faith and a solid belief in *Gott*, maybe Ben could make a difference for her, too.

It was something to think about.

Chapter Six

Caroline picked up a plate from the drying rack and swiped both sides with a clean towel before setting the dish aside. It was late afternoon and it had been a long, tiring day. First, they'd prepared approximately three hundred sandwiches, cupcakes and noodles to feed the *familye* and friends attending the funeral. The service had lasted two and a half hours. Then there was the graveside service. As the nearest living relatives, Caroline and her *familye* had remained beside the graves until the pallbearers had completely buried the two coffins. When they'd returned to the house, the long tables had been replenished with food by the other women in the *Gmay*. But Caroline wasn't very hungry. She reminded herself that death was a part of life and she must accept *Gott's* will, but it wasn't easy.

By three o'clock, the tables, benches and songbooks had been packed away inside the bench wagons and hauled away. Through it all, Ben Yoder was right there, helping the other men. Thank goodness for the members of their *Gmay*, who had pitched in willingly to help with the work.

Over the past week, there had been a nonstop flow of men and women coming in to assist with farm chores and clean the house and barn from floor to ceiling. The outpouring of love from her *Gmay* reminded Caroline how much she loved her faith and that she was never alone, no matter what trials she must face in this life.

Gazing out the kitchen window, she listened quietly to the muted voices around her as the women finished washing the dishes. Across the cow pasture, she saw a line of horse-drawn buggies marching along the county road in single file. The entire Amish community of Riverton and many members from the Westcliffe *Gmay* had come to the cemetery, even though they hadn't known the deceased. It didn't matter. Anna and James had been two of their own, and they wouldn't abandon them or their children in their time of need.

In tandem, the line of buggies had followed the two hearse wagons, which carried the earthly remains of James and Anna Bontrager. Each buggy was overly crowded with large families, but no one minded. This was a time for love and introspection as they all considered the living hope and salvation Christ provided each of them.

Caroline glanced over at the table. Little Mary sat alone, picking at a piece of shoofly pie. Even the rich molasses, cinnamon and brown sugar couldn't tempt her to take a full bite. The girl looked so small and defenseless, sitting there in her black dress, apron and shawl. The *familye* was in mourning and would wear nothing but black for the next year. Since they'd arrived at the house several days earlier, neither child had eaten much. But starting tomorrow, Caroline was determined to make that change. After all, she was their cousin as well as their teacher. She was obligated to look after them and intended to do just that.

Lifting her head, Caroline gazed out the window again. Seth stood leaning against the corral gate, staring off into space. As usual, he was all by himself. And though he seemed to have formed an attachment to Ben, the boy was overly quiet and sullen. Caroline figured that was to be expected but hoped it would change once the boy started attending school next week.

As she watched, Caroline saw Ben walk over to the boy and rest a hand on Seth's shoulder. The child didn't reject the silent comfort Ben offered. But maybe Ben wasn't the best person to be comforting Seth. With Ben's past, Caroline certainly didn't think he represented a good example for the child. Maybe she should intercede. Maybe she should…

"Those two sure are a pair. The poor dears."

Caroline glanced over and found Sarah Yoder standing beside her. The woman followed her gaze and nodded at Seth and Ben.

"What do you mean?" Caroline asked.

Sarah shrugged. "Ben wasn't much older than Seth when he lost both his parents. If anyone can relate to what Seth and Mary are going through, it's Ben," Sarah said.

Oh. Caroline had heard a few rumblings about Ben's parents but hadn't given it much thought. Had he been overly quiet and hostile following the deaths of his parents? No doubt he had felt lost and all alone, just like Seth. Caroline felt a stab of compassion for what he must have suffered in his life. But that was no excuse to kill a man later on.

"I think it's important to teach Mary and Seth to accept *Gott's* will and not to fight it. I hope they can learn to have a calm, peaceful heart. Even though their parents are gone, they must go on living," Caroline said.

"I hope so, too. But those are not easy lessons to learn at such a young age. Ben can attest to that. I have no doubt he can impart his wisdom to Seth, and the boy would be better off for it." With those words, Sarah reached for a large clean casserole dish and set it on the table beside her wicker basket. The dish must belong to her and she wanted to take it home when she departed.

Caroline thought about what the bishop's wife had told her. No doubt she cared a great deal for Ben. After all, the man lived in her house and was her nephew by marriage. But Caroline wasn't sure she approved of Ben's friendship with Seth. The boy was quiet and respectful, but he was also young and impressionable. She would prefer he had a better example to follow. Someone like Uncle Mervin or Bishop Yoder.

But then she reconsidered. Ben had been nothing but kind and respectful to her. And she couldn't fault his dedication to hard work. Over the past eighteen months since she'd first met him, he'd never done anything to indicate he had a foul temper. Not once.

But he'd still killed a man. Surely, his anger was there, buried deep inside him. She was certain of it.

"Caroline?"

She looked down and found Mary standing beside her, holding her plate and fork. As Caroline took the dish from the girl, she noticed she'd barely touched her food.

"*Ja*, sweetums?" Caroline longed to bend down and meet the girl's eyes but still couldn't manage that movement.

"Where is our *heemet*? Where will we live now?" Mary asked.

"You'll live here with us, of course." Aunt Hannah spoke from nearby, her voice a bit wobbly with emotion. This had been a difficult day for all of them, and she was trying hard to be upbeat for the children's benefit.

"This isn't our *heemet*!"

Caroline jerked toward the open doorway. Seth had spoken. He stood beside Ben. They must have just returned to the house. The boy's hands were clenched and his face was red with anger.

"We were gonna buy our own farm to live on. But our *mamm* and *daed* are dead. We don't belong anywhere now," Seth said. Before anyone could respond, he dashed outside toward the barn, rudely brushing past several people as he went.

Along with Aunt Hannah and Ben, Caroline stared after the boy in surprise. She'd never heard such a rude outburst, yet she couldn't be angry at him. He had every right to be distraught. But he needed to learn respect and that death was not the end, but rather the beginning.

"Oh, dear. He seems quite upset," Aunt Hannah said, looking red and flustered.

"Don't worry. I'll speak with him," Ben said.

Without waiting for their approval, he hurried after the child, his long stride so strong and confident. Caroline wondered again if he was the best person to talk with Seth about death and eternal salvation. Though Seth had lost so much, this was a teaching moment. The child needed to be taught acceptance and reverence. He needed to understand that *Gott's* will must supersede his own. That hope and faith must be exercised at all times, even during the darkest ones such as this. And he needed to learn that such outbursts of emotion were not acceptable in the Amish faith.

Could Ben translate these beliefs to Seth in a satisfactory, calm manner? Caroline had her doubts.

Ben wasn't sure what he was going to say to Seth. As he entered the dim interior of the barn, he blinked and glanced around, looking for the boy. He found him in one of the empty animal stalls, sitting on a bale of hay, facing the wall.

Looping his thumbs around his black suspenders, Ben paused and considered his words carefully. Memories washed over him of the day his mother had died, followed by his father less than a year later. And he knew there was nothing he could say to ease the hurt. But maybe he could provide a bit of comfort.

"Seth, we need to talk," he began in a gentle voice.

The boy hunched his shoulders, the only indication that he'd heard him. As Ben stepped nearer, he blocked the exit out of the stall. He hadn't planned it this way, but if Seth made a break for it, there was no way out except through him. The boy would have to listen to him. For now. And yet, Ben didn't want to be stern. After his parents died, he'd been treated harshly and it had done nothing but alienate him. It had made everything worse.

Deciding to be gentle, Ben stepped inside the stall and sat beside the boy on the bale of hay.

"First, I want you to know that none of this is your fault. And it's not Mary's fault, either. Things just happen sometimes," Ben said.

He paused, letting that sink in. He remembered how he'd thought he'd done something bad to cause his parents' deaths and knew it would have made a difference if someone had told him it wasn't his fault.

"Second, I know what it feels like to lose your *eldre* when you are young. I lost my *mudder* when I was seven and my *vadder* just after I turned eight," he continued.

Seth looked up at him, his mouth dropping open in surprise. "Did they die in a bus crash like my folks?"

Ben shook his head. "*Ne*, my *mamm* died of cancer. And I think losing my *mudder* when she was so young was what killed my *daed*, even though the doctor said it was a heart attack. I believe my *vadder* died of a broken heart. But either way, I was left all alone in the world with no *familye* of my own."

The boy sat up straighter. Ben realized he had caught Seth's attention.

"You didn't even have a *schweschder* or *bruder*?"

"*Ne*, not even a brother or sister."

"What did you do?" Seth asked.

"I went on living. My *onkel* Grant took me in to his *heemet* to live with him and then, almost two years ago, I moved here to Colorado to live with my *onkel* Amos."

"But he's not your *daed*," Seth said.

"*Ne*, but he's been awfully *gut* to me and I love him dearly. It's always best to be with your *familye*. They share your same heritage and beliefs."

"Do you like living here in Colorado?" Seth asked.

Ben ducked his head, considering the question. Did he like it here?

"I'm not sure. It's as *gut* as any place, I suppose. I'm grateful to my extended *familye* for taking me in, but it's not the same. More than anything, I'd like to have a *familye* of my own. A place that I can really call home. But I know my *aent* and *onkel* love me. I'll always have a place to belong with them."

Wow! He'd just confessed more out loud to this little boy of six years than he'd been willing to admit even to himself. But he didn't want to give the impression that it was all bad. In that moment Caroline's words of faith entered his mind and he knew what he should say.

"I feel blessed to be a part of our faith and to be with people who care for me. You still have your sister and she's depending on you. No matter what, you still have a *familye*. You'll want to always take care of Mary. Your *mamm* and *daed* are depending on you. They would expect nothing less. And the Lord expects it, too. I don't presume to know all of His ways, but I do know He walks beside us no matter what hardships we might face. With *Gott*, you're never alone, Seth. I hope you really believe that," Ben said.

Seth bowed his head, as if thinking this over. "I don't know. It's not the same now."

"I know, you're right. But I've learned that love and service continue even after our *mamm* and *daed* are gone from our lives. It's a test of sorts. To see if we will learn how to serve and love others," Ben said.

"Is that what you did?" Seth asked.

"I try to serve others whenever I can. But I trust in *Gott* that I'll one day have a wife and *familye* of my own. And you'll hopefully have that, too." As he said the words, Ben prayed what he said would come true.

A small sound came from behind them, and Ben turned. Caroline stood in the open doorway of the barn. At first glance, her cheeks went bright pink and he knew she'd been eavesdropping. A blaze of mortification heated him from the neck up. How much had she overheard? What must she think of him now?

"I... I'm sorry. I didn't mean to interrupt. I just wanted to make sure Seth was okay," she said.

"I'm fine. You don't need to check on me all the time." Seth stood and edged toward the door. The angry expression had returned and it was obvious he felt embarrassed, too. The boy had let down his guard for a few minutes with Ben and seemed angry that Caroline had witnessed it.

"It was kind of you to check on him. But Seth is *allrecht* now. And I think we're finished here if you need the barn," Ben said, trying to be polite and show by example how Seth should act.

Without a word or backward glance, Seth fled the barn. In the silent aftermath, Ben walked over to Caroline and gazed down at her face. Tears glimmered in her eyes and she brushed them away, obviously struggling not to lose her hold on her crutches. At the cemetery, she'd been walking with just one crutch, and he thought she was getting stronger every day. But now her face was drained of color, her eyes clouded with pain and grief. From the droop of her shoulders, he could tell she was exhausted. And little wonder. It had been a difficult week for her and her *familye*.

"*Danke* for speaking with Seth," she said.

"It was my pleasure. I just hope it helps. Were you very close to Anna and James?" he asked.

She nodded and licked her upper lip. "*Ja*, I've known them both all my life. Anna and I were very close when I lived in Ohio, and I'll miss her and James very much."

Her voice spiked and he could tell she was overcome by emotion. A fresh welling of moisture filled her eyes and ran down her cheeks. Before he could think to stop himself, Ben reached out and wiped one tear away. Caroline stared up at him, her lips slightly parted. How he hated to see her cry.

"I'm so sorry. I wish I could do something to change this outcome," he said.

"There's nothing anyone can do. We just need to exercise faith and keep on living. We have Mary and Seth to think about now." She turned away, breaking the special moment between them.

He followed as she made her way back to the house. She stumbled several times, attesting that she'd over-exerted herself today. Each time, he was there to hold her arm until she could regain her footing. And once he had her inside the house, he whispered a few words to Hannah, who insisted Caroline should sit down for the rest of the evening.

Soon afterward Ben took his departure. Caroline was right. The funeral was over with and they had to go on living. School was back in session, and there was much work to be done there and also on his uncle's farm.

But Ben wished Caroline hadn't overheard what he'd said to Seth. It was too personal. Too painful. And he didn't want her to think any less of him than she already did.

Chapter Seven

Two weeks later Caroline and her *familye* had settled into a routine. Ben picked her up each morning and drove her to school. Her aunt and uncle had integrated Seth and Mary into their daily chores and conducted their affairs like nothing had disrupted their lives. Hannah was so busy raising her own seven children that she didn't have time to coddle two more kids who were grieving for their parents. Caroline had naturally stepped in, spending extra time reading and comforting the two orphans. But no matter what she or others did, Seth grew more sullen and distant, seeming to withdraw into himself. He didn't willingly participate at school and he only spoke when absolutely necessary. Even little Mary, who was having occasional nightmares, was worried about her big brother. He never played with her anymore and had even started pinching her and pulling her hair. Needless to say, Caroline was worried about the boy.

"He's disappeared again." Hannah came in the back door to the farmhouse, carrying the kitchen garbage can. The screen door clapped closed behind her as she set the can down with a loud thump.

Caroline sat at the table, tallying a list of numbers in her grade book. It was early morning and she had just finished her grading before Ben would pick her up for school. The table was set for breakfast, and she had cleared a little space to work. Caroline and her aunt had prepared several pans of food, which sat warming on the stove, waiting for the children to finish their farm chores before they came inside to eat. The air smelled of sausage and eggs, fresh-baked biscuits and home-made strawberry preserves. The *familye* had been up since four o'clock that morning.

"Who's disappeared?" Caroline asked, jotting a final number at the bottom of her notebook before she snapped the book closed and slid it into her schoolbag.

"Seth, that's who. I asked that boy to dump the garbage can over an hour ago and now I can't find him anywhere. Anytime I ask him to do something, he just ignores me and I end up doing it myself. I hate to say it, but I'm afraid that boy is downright lazy. I don't know what to do with him." Hannah raised her hands in exasperation and released a big huff of air.

Caroline understood her aunt's frustration. The Amish were extremely hard workers and couldn't abide idleness or disobedience of any kind. They relied on every member of the *familye*, including the little children, to help with the tasks. That was what it took for a large *familye* like this to earn a living and survive. Seth's defiance had become a huge problem for them.

"Maybe I can find him." Pushing back from the

table, Caroline clasped her elbow crutch and stood with minimal effort. Walking was getting much easier, and she thought she'd soon be able to trade the crutch for a cane.

Hannah released a sarcastic laugh as she picked up a dish towel. "I've already looked and looked. You won't be able to find him. Not unless he wants to be found. I've spent the last ten minutes calling for him. I'm ready to have your uncle take the rod to him."

Caroline cringed. The thought of Uncle Mervin beating Seth with a rod of hickory made her stomach churn. Seth had lost so much already. She couldn't stand the thought of striking him for disobedience and was determined to get to the bottom of this.

"I'll find him." She spoke with a confidence she didn't really feel.

Ignoring her aunt's pursed lips, she stepped outside on the back porch. Sunshine blazed across the yard. Levi, her ten-year-old cousin, stood in the pigpen, dumping slop into the feeding trough. Alice, his older sister, was helping secure the gate so the pigs didn't escape. Joseph and even five-year-old Benuel were in the chicken coop gathering eggs and feeding the chickens. Everyone was busy doing their chores, except Seth. So where was he? And why on earth was he hiding again?

Caroline's intuition told her something was very wrong here. She didn't think Seth was lazy. This was a bigger problem. She'd noticed Seth disappeared from time to time, but only when he was asked to dump the garbage. So what was amiss?

Standing beside the corrals, she scanned the open

yard, trying to imagine where she might hide if she were a six-year-old boy. A quick scan of the tall elm tree branches in the yard told her he wasn't up there. The obvious choice was the barn, but surely, Aunt Hannah had checked there already. But maybe she'd missed a small nook or cranny where the little boy might go unnoticed.

Shuffling along on the crutch, Caroline walked through the barn, peering into every dark corner.

"Seth! Where are you?" she called over and over again as she walked along.

No response. Not a single sound.

She crossed to the back of the barn and peered outside. Uncle Mervin had already milked and fed the cows and draft horses before turning them out into the south pasture. He was now out back, burning their garbage in a tall canister. Red flames flickered above the metal rim, consuming a variety of paper refuse. What Uncle Mervin couldn't burn, he tossed into the compost pile to use as fertilizer on their fields. They wasted very little on this farm.

Still, Caroline caught no sign of Seth. But he must be here somewhere.

With the pungent scent of smoke filling her nostrils, she stepped back inside the barn. Standing in the shadows, she held perfectly still and listened intently. After a few minutes she heard the slightest rustling just overhead. Several strands of hay wafted through the air and fell to the ground.

Hmm. Someone was up there. She thought she'd finally found Seth's hiding place.

"Seth," she called in a quiet, gentle tone. "Can you

please come down from the hayloft now? It's almost time to go to school and you haven't had your breakfast yet."

She waited, hoping he wouldn't make her climb up after him. Because frankly, she wasn't sure she could physically do it, and she didn't want to fetch Mary or one of the other children to come and get him down.

He finally obeyed, peering over the edge of the loft. He had the good grace to look sheepish as he climbed down the wooden ladder. When he stood directly in front of her, she reached out slowly and plucked several pieces of straw away from his hair and clothes, then rested her hand on his slender shoulder.

"Seth, I know this is tough and I know you're angry that your parents aren't here. But when you want to run away, can you draw me a picture instead?" she asked.

His eyebrows drew together in a frown of confusion and he glanced at her. "What for?"

"So I can see what you're feeling inside. I'll leave some paper and crayons for you in the living room. You can draw what you're feeling right on the piece of paper. But no more running away and hiding. Otherwise, we'll be worried that you're in danger. Okay?"

He gave a noncommittal shrug. "Okay."

She smiled. "*Gut*. Now, can you tell me why you didn't dump the garbage can again?"

No answer. He just stared at the ground, silent as a tomb.

"*Komm* with me and I'll show you what needs to be done next time Aunt Hannah asks," she said.

She turned and headed toward the back of the barn where Uncle Mervin was burning garbage. The wind carried the strong smell of smoke on the air. Seth followed for three steps but then stopped dead in his tracks. As he gazed at the burning barrel, his eyes widened and his face contorted in a look of absolute terror. And before Caroline could say or do anything to help the boy, he turned and ran screaming toward the house.

"Seth!" she cried, trying to follow him, but she just wasn't fast enough.

He disappeared inside the house, slamming the door behind him so hard that the entire structure seemed to shake on its foundation.

By the time Caroline made it inside, Aunt Hannah was sitting at the kitchen table feeding the baby and looking completely bewildered.

The screaming continued as the boy pounded up the stairs to his bedroom. The slamming of the door told Caroline that he didn't want any intruders.

"What on earth is going on? Is Seth hurt?" Aunt Hannah asked, coming to her feet.

"*Ne*, not the way you think. I can't explain right now, but I think I've figured out what's wrong with him. I'll take care of it." Caroline shuffled through the room and made her way upstairs.

It took her a few moments to climb the stairs. She paused at the top of the landing, trying to catch her breath. Seth's screaming had stopped but she could hear his muffled crying on the other side of the door. Lifting her hand, she knocked gently, hoping the portal wasn't locked.

"Seth? May I *komm* in?" she called in a calm voice. No response.

Turning the knob, she stepped inside. Seth had curled up on his bed, his head buried beneath a pillow.

Caroline sat next to him but was careful not to touch him.

"Seth, I think I know why you don't want to empty the garbage can. It's because of the fire, isn't it?" she said.

He didn't speak but his body went more rigid, telling her she was right.

"When your *mamm* and *daed* died, there was a fire, wasn't there?" she asked.

She waited, giving him plenty of time to think. As a teacher, she'd discovered that it took her students several seconds to digest what she'd asked them and come back with a response. So she paused now, exercising lots of patience. Finally, he pulled his head out from beneath the pillow and sat up, but he didn't meet her gaze.

"There was a fire, wasn't there?" she asked again, just in case he'd forgotten the question.

He nodded and she almost breathed a sigh of relief. Finally, they were getting somewhere. She reminded herself that both Seth and Mary had been on the bus with their parents when the semi-truck had plowed into them. And she was ashamed of herself for not asking him about what had happened. The Amish were a stoic people who didn't mollycoddle their children. But neither did Caroline think it was good for Seth to keep the experience bottled up inside. Maybe talking about it would help make things easier.

She touched his hand, just to see if he might let her hug him. But he pulled away. She didn't push but she made him a promise.

"*Ach*, I can tell you this. You don't have to empty the

garbage can ever again, nor do you have to go out by the burning barrel anymore. Okay?" she said.

He looked up at her, his eyes filled with giant crocodile tears that ran unheeded down his cheeks. He looked so sad and forlorn that she felt inspired to pull him into her arms. If he fought her, she'd release him immediately. But above all else, she didn't want to force this traumatized child into doing anything he didn't want to do.

He curled into her arms and held on tight, and she released a satisfied sigh.

"You know, whenever I'm upset about something, I have a little scripture from the Bible that I repeat in my mind and it helps me feel better every time. Maybe you'd like to try it out?" she suggested.

He didn't answer. Didn't move a muscle. But he didn't refuse her offer, either, and she took that as approval.

"Peace I leave with you, my peace I give unto you: not as the world giveth, give I unto you. Let not your heart be troubled, neither let it be afraid."

She paused, letting it sink in.

"Do you know who said those words?" she asked.

He shook his head, listening intently.

"It was Jesus Christ, our Savior. The passage is found in the Book of John." She reached over to the bedside table and retrieved a Bible. After flipping it open, she handed the book to him and pointed out the exact verse.

"Perhaps, whenever you're feeling upset, you might like to repeat that scripture in your mind and feel the Lord close to you, offering His support. Do you think you might like to do that?" she asked.

He nodded, taking the book onto his lap and tracing the verse with his fingertip.

Downstairs, she heard a knock on the back door and thought Ben must have arrived to take her to school. But still, she sat with Seth for several more minutes, until she knew he was calm again. Then she stood.

"You and Mary are going to be *allrecht*, Seth. I promise you. Just trust in the Lord. And I'm always here any time you need to talk."

He didn't acknowledge her words, but she knew he'd heard her.

"Now, hurry and get ready. I want you to have your breakfast so you can do *gut* work in school today. I'll expect you to do your best," she said.

She wasn't a psychologist or trained in dealing with childhood trauma, but she sensed that both Seth and Mary needed lots of love and understanding right now. But they also needed to understand her expectations. And before she left for the day, she was going to make sure that both Aunt Hannah and Uncle Mervin knew that Seth was absolutely terrified of fire. Not because he might be burned, but because there had been a fire the night his parents had died in that horrible accident. And until he could cope with their deaths, she didn't want to push the boy beyond what he could stand.

As she slid her elbow crutch in front of her and stepped out of the room, she hoped and prayed she'd said and done the right things today. Because she knew that helping Seth recover from this trauma was going to take patience and time. And as soon as the school day was over, she was going to pay a short visit to Becca

Graber. Becca had substitute-taught for Caroline last school year. And though neither woman was formally trained in dealing with an issue like this, Becca had studied quite a lot so she could help her soon-to-be step-son, Sam, when the boy stopped speaking following the deaths of his mother and two sisters. Maybe Becca could offer some insight into how Caroline could help Seth and Mary.

"Caroline?"

She looked down and saw Aunt Hannah standing at the bottom of the stairs. She held baby Susan in her arms. The little girl was teething and overly fussy and had kept Hannah up most of the night. Hannah looked tired and overwhelmed.

"Ben is here to take you to school," Hannah said.

Caroline nodded. "I'll be right there."

"Is everything *allrecht* with Seth? Is he hurt?" Hannah asked, looking worried.

"*Ne*, he's fine for now," Caroline said.

As quickly as possible, she negotiated the stairs and quietly explained to her aunt what had happened.

"Oh, dear. What can I do?" Hannah asked.

"Just give him a different chore. Maybe he could gather the eggs instead and Levi could dump the gar-bage for the time being," Caroline said.

"*Ach*, of course." Hannah nodded.

Caroline hugged her aunt, offering her some reas-surance, too. Then she turned to gather up her bookbag and went outside to greet Ben. She didn't know why but this morning's events had made her want to talk to him. In spite of his reputation, he had a soothing way about him that always made her feel at ease. He was just a plain Amish man and didn't know how to handle a child suffering over the traumatic deaths of his parents, and yet Ben always seemed to know the right thing to say.

And that realization confused Caroline more than ever. Because she didn't want to be around Ben any more than necessary. But he might be able to help with Seth, too.

Ben sat on the porch swing and crossed his ankles as he waited for Caroline. Sitting in front of Becca Graber's house, he enjoyed the way the afternoon sunlight glimmered through the treetops. Instead of verdant green, the leaves had changed to a light, lemon color. Soon, the weather would get colder and the leaves would turn orange and brown and fall to the ground.

He'd been momentarily surprised when Caroline had sat next to him in the buggy that morning and explained Seth's problem. She'd asked him to drive her over to Becca Graber's house as soon as school was out, so she could speak with the woman about possible solutions. Eager to be of service, Ben had agreed.

Caroline wasn't inside very long. Ben straightened when the door to the little log farmhouse swung open and she stepped outside with Becca on her heels.

A rather thick book was tucked beneath one of Caroline's arms. Because she was struggling to walk with her elbow crutch, he quickly stepped forward and took the book before it could fall to the ground.

"*Hallo* Ben," Becca greeted him with a bright smile.

Tugging on the brim of his black felt hat, he nodded respectfully. "Ma'am."

"I think you're on the right track," Becca said to Caroline. "Giving Seth a scripture to memorize and repeat in his mind every time he gets upset and letting him draw his feelings on paper was a very smart move. I'm sure it'll help him a lot."

They'd reached the buggy, and Ben opened the door and set the book on the front seat.

"I hope so. I didn't know what else to do. *Danke* for all your great ideas. I'll be sure to read the book and then implement some techniques to help both Seth and Mary," Caroline said.

She turned and hugged Becca, then did something that completely took Ben offguard. She slid her arm brace onto the floor of the buggy, then reached for his hand to support her as she climbed inside.

"You're so kind to help Caroline like this. I'm really glad you're here for her. She told me how blessed she is to have you as her assistant," Becca told him.

The praise felt alien to Ben. The Amish weren't given to fawning over anyone except the Lord. But he admitted—only to himself—that her words pleased him enormously. Mostly because he thought everyone in his *Gmay* disliked him.

Becca stepped back and Ben closed the door.

"Goodbye!" Becca said before turning back toward the house.

Ben paused, his mouth dropping open in surprise. Caroline had told her she was blessed to have his help? Because the buggy door was closed, he didn't think Caroline had heard Becca's words, but they touched his heart like nothing else could.

"Danke. Mach's gut," he called to Becca.

From the windshield, Caroline waved to her friend as Ben hurried to climb into the driver's seat. Taking the leather lead lines into his hands, he released the brake and slapped the lines lightly against the horse's back. The animal jerked forward and off they went.

"Did Becca have some *gut* ideas for you?" he asked after they'd been driving for several moments.

"*Ja*, she's so knowledgeable. She makes me think that maybe I'm not the right person to be teaching the scholars of our school. They need Becca. She's older and so much more experienced than I am," Caroline said.

He snorted. "That's because she taught them last year. But I've watched you with the kids and you know just as much. You've simply come across an unusual issue that needs dealing with. But look at you! You're going the extra mile to find out how to help Seth and Mary. They're blessed to have such a caring teacher as you. And besides, Becca is marrying Jesse King in another month. She'll have her own *familye* to care for soon enough and can't teach anymore."

Caroline looked at him, her expression one of surprise. He hoped he hadn't said anything inappropriate. His words had been chosen out of respect and support, not an attempt to upset or disappoint her.

"*Danke*, Ben. I appreciate your kind words, more than I can say. You've been more than generous and I appreciate it," she said.

He stared straight ahead, trying not to show a big, silly smile. But inside, he was grinning like a fool. He'd tried to say the right things and she'd turned it about and made him feel good.

As he drove her home, Caroline rattled off several

ideas Becca had given her to help Seth and Mary. And it occurred to Ben that Caroline had never been this chatty around him before. Which told him she was starting to become more comfortable with him.

"The first thing I want to do is get Seth and Mary to start drawing pictures for me," she said, her voice filled with discovery. "Then we can discuss them. Mary hasn't been acting out but I'm wondering if we should nip some problems in the bud now, before it catches up to her. She has had a few nightmares and I don't want things to get worse. Don't you agree?"

He coughed, stunned that she would ask for his opinion.

"*Ja*, I think that would be wise," he said.

"Of course, *Aent* Hannah and *Onkel* Mervin should be included in everything I'm doing with the kids. They'll be raising Seth and Mary now and need to know how to handle certain situations."

She picked up the heavy book that Becca had given her and thumbed through some of the pages. "*Ach*, I suppose I'll be up late reading tonight."

She smiled, and Ben thought he hadn't seen her this happy since before her buggy accident. It was nice.

She continued to talk and bounce ideas off him. Her acumen surprised him, and he simply nodded and agreed with what she proposed. After all, what did a big, gruff Amish man like him know about helping a child overcome a traumatic experience? He hadn't yet gotten over his own bad childhood and felt completely inept.

"*Danke*, Ben," Caroline said when he parked in front of her home and helped her out of the buggy.

He assisted her inside and returned her wave, then

got back in the buggy and pulled out of the yard. And during his ride home, he had plenty of time to puzzle over Caroline and her zest for life. She was like a hound with a bone now. Seth and Mary needed her help, and she was determined to do whatever was necessary to make them happy again.

Ben wasn't surprised. Since the moment he'd met Caroline, he'd known she was an amazing, wonderful woman. All others paled in comparison to her. And once more, he regretted his past and wished their situation could be so much different.

But the reality wouldn't budge, and dwelling on what could have been did neither of them any good at all.

Chapter Eight

"Teacher Caroline. Come quick! The *buwe* are fighting."

Caroline looked up from where she sat on the front steps of the school. Little Mary had run around the corner of the building, her eyes wide and her face creased with worry.

Coretta and Annie, two girls from the fourth-grade class, sat on either side of Caroline. She'd been teaching them how to do a double crochet stitch. A wicker basket of dark purple yarn sat beside her, and she held a crochet needle and a half-finished dishcloth in her lap. The girls were making hot pot holders, hanging dish towels and dishcloths as a surprise for their mothers.

The screams and yelling of recess permeated Caroline's consciousness. She'd been concentrating so hard on counting stitches that she hadn't noticed how frenzied and shrill the sounds had become.

Looking out at the playground, she realized some of the kids were playing at the side of the schoolhouse and she couldn't see them from her vantage point. But now that she listened, she realized she wasn't hearing the happy cries of children at play. No, these were angry sounds.

After setting the dishcloth and needle inside the basket, she clasped her elbow crutch and pushed herself up. The girls rushed to take her arms and help her stand. And once she found her footing, she shuffled forward as she followed Mary.

When she rounded the corner of the schoolhouse, the shrieks became louder and Caroline couldn't believe what she saw. Seth and Caleb Yoder grappled around in the dirt, hitting and punching one another in the face and torso. Several other children stood around them, looking horrified and fretful. Elmer Albrecht, who was the oldest boy in the school, was trying to pull the two boys apart and demanding they stop, to no avail. The two fighting boys were so angry, their expressions filled with such hate, that they didn't seem to hear or see anything but each other.

"Schtopp!" Caroline called as she hurried over to intercede.

The gawking children parted the way for her, but Seth and Caleb didn't quit punching each other. They didn't even acknowledge her presence. They continued to hit and kick as Caroline endeavored to push her way between them.

"Oww!" she cried when one fist connected firmly with her jaw.

Her face exploded with pain, and the impact knocked her backward. She felt herself falling. Before the ground slammed up to meet her, strong hands caught her and set her back on her feet.

"Are you *allrecht*?"

Ben! As usual, he'd come to her rescue.

He restored the crutch to her hands, and she stood there shaking and gripping the handle so hard that her knuckles turned white. She gasped for breath, trying to ignore the pulsing pain in her face. Her legs trembled like gelatin and she rubbed her aching jaw. She knew that Ben had been working in the back, putting the last of the playground equipment together. And she'd never been so happy to see him in all her life. What if he hadn't been here?

"*Ja*, I'm okay. But the boys!" she cried, desperate to stop the fight.

With a satisfied nod, he turned and she saw something she'd never seen before. As Ben faced the two recalcitrant boys, a horrible emotion flared across his face. It was dark and ferocious and turned his normally calm expression into one of absolute fury. His wide shoulders tensed and his eyes narrowed to dangerous black points as his jaw hardened like a block of granite. From the time they were in the cradle, Amish children were taught that fighting was unacceptable. It went against everything they believed in. It brought nothing but heartache. The Amish were pacifists and never used force. No, not ever. And after what had happened to Ben, Caroline figured he understood that principle better than any of them.

"That's enough!" Ben roared.

Caroline flinched. Several little girls clung to her in fear. They watched as Ben took each boy by the arm and pulled them apart. He didn't hurt them, but they couldn't escape his solid grip. Like ravening wolves, they wriggled and fought to get at each other again, and Caroline thought she had never seen such atrocious behavior in all her life.

"Schtopp!" Ben thundered once more at the two boys.

Finally, Seth and Caleb came to their senses and stopped struggling. As if realizing the trouble they were in, they cowered and hung their heads, their argument suddenly forgotten.

"What do you think you're doing?" Ben spoke in *Deitsch*, his voice low and dangerous.

Neither boy spoke. They just stared at him with absolute contrition. And yet, Caroline saw something in Seth that she'd never seen in one of her students before. A sullen resentment glimmered in his eyes. The boy was far from cowed. He wanted to hurt Caleb. To kick, hit and punch the other boy. And she realized helping him overcome the trauma of his parents' deaths wasn't going to be as easy as she thought.

Caroline watched Ben carefully, wondering what he might do. In those few short moments, she'd received an inkling of what he must have been like when he'd killed a man. Cruel and ferocious. And yet, he seemed completely in control of his actions. Just as she imagined Jesus must have been when he chased the money changers out of His father's temple.

Ben always seemed so gentle. So considerate and kind. But seeing him like this made her realize that everyone had a dark side. And it frightened Caroline more than she could say.

"Do you not know that fighting is forbidden? Jesus taught us to turn the other cheek. Do you think He would approve of what you've done here today?" he asked the boys.

They didn't respond, but Seth's face darkened. He didn't appear repentant at all. Not in the least.

"And you struck Teacher Caroline, too. How dare you do such a thing? You owe her your respect. You should be protecting her, not hitting her," Ben said.

Both boys glanced at Caroline, their arms still firmly held in Ben's grasp.

"I'm sorry for fighting. I didn't mean to hit you, Teacher Caroline," Caleb said, his eyes filled with tears.

"I'm sorry for hitting you, too. I… I didn't mean for you to get hurt," Seth said.

But Seth hadn't apologized for fighting. A terrible, blinding energy emanated from the boy, telling her he was still filled with rage. He wanted to fight. He wanted to scream and kill something. She could hardly comprehend such a harsh emotion. And for the first time since she'd been back at her teaching job, she felt like she was in over her head. She hadn't been able to stop the fight. If Ben hadn't been here today, she didn't know what she would have done. The situation could have escalated and been so much worse. Someone could have gotten seriously hurt. And what would the parents and school board say when they found out?

Ben released the two boys and stood back, his expression completely calm but still stern. For Caroline, it was like watching the night turn to day. One moment Ben was like a brick wall, filled with such power and enmity that she was stunned by his energy. And the next moment he was perfectly still. All Caroline could wonder was, who was this man?

He came to stand beside her, as if waiting for her to take charge now that the situation was under control. Caroline coughed to clear her voice and tried to regain her composure. Ignoring the ache in her jaw, she stepped forward.

"Students, I would like all of you to return to the classroom now. Recess is over. I want you to study quietly in your workbooks. Caleb and Seth, you will remain here for the time being," she said, her voice vibrating slightly.

All of the other children returned to the schoolhouse. Once the other kids were inside, Caroline faced Seth and Caleb again. She was highly conscious of Ben remaining right where he was, like a silent bodyguard watching over her. And she wasn't sure if that was good or bad.

"I'm so disappointed in you boys today," she began, grateful that her voice sounded much calmer. "You both know better than to fight. Your parents will be told about this and there will be a punishment forthcoming, once I figure out what that should be."

"I don't have any parents!" Seth shouted, his eyes filled with angry tears.

Oh, dear. Caroline cringed, wishing she'd chosen a better word. She hadn't thought before she opened her mouth. Her heart ached for all that this child had lost. She wanted to go easy on him but knew the bishop and her aunt and uncle wouldn't approve if she didn't do something to impress upon the two boys' minds the importance of what she was trying to teach. No fighting. Period.

"I'm sorry, Seth. I misspoke. But you do have a *fami-lye* here that loves you very much. And there are parents in your *heemet*. You have us. Remember you were going to draw a picture and recite a scripture whenever you were feeling angry or upset? Did you forget about that?" she asked.

Seth's face darkened, his hands clenched as he glared at Caroline and Ben. "I didn't forget. But you're not my *mudder* and *vadder*. They're dead!"

He turned and sprinted toward the school. A sense of panic swept over Caroline. If the boy ran away, she didn't have the physical strength to chase after him. And she really didn't want to ask Ben to do it. She watched in relief as Seth pounded up the steps and entered the schoolhouse, slamming the door behind him. He was still very angry, but at least he'd stayed here. He was safe for now. But she needed time to think how to handle the situation. Once he calmed down, she'd ask him to draw a picture. She must be consistent and not deviate from her plans to help him. Otherwise, she'd lose him for sure.

"Please return to the classroom," she told Caleb in a very soft voice.

The boy ducked his head. "I'm so sorry, Teacher Caroline. We were just playing a game and he dropped a pocketknife. I picked it up and handed it back to him and he blew up at me. I... I'm sorry I fought back. I know I shouldn't have. And it won't happen ever again. I promise."

A pocketknife! It wasn't so odd to have such a thing at school. Many of the boys helped cut willows and liked to whittle on sticks. The Amish school didn't have a "no weapons policy" like the *Englisch* schools did, mostly because it had never been an issue before. Even though the Amish were pacifists, they all had guns and knives and hunted for food to feed their families. But why would Caleb's touching the knife be cause for Seth to attack him?

She heard the true remorse in Caleb's words and nodded. "*Gut*, I'm glad to hear that. But you should also apologize to Seth, once he's calmed down a little. And I'll expect you to never fight again."

Caleb nodded solemnly, then jogged back to the schoolhouse. Caroline breathed a heavy sigh and looked at Ben. She hated to go back inside the classroom and try to continue their lessons. There was such a feeling of contention in the air. Even the other children who hadn't been fighting must surely feel it. Everyone was highly upset.

"It'll be *allrecht*." Ben gave her a gentle smile of encouragement.

How did he always seem to know what she was thinking?

"I'll be nearby if you need me," he said before turning and walking away.

She watched as he disappeared around the back of the school and knew he'd be listening for any sounds of trouble inside. On the one hand, she was glad to have him here. She hated to admit it, but Bishop Yoder had been wise to send Ben here to help her out this year. Yet, on the other hand, she wondered if he was a good influence on the kids. After all, he'd fought back, and look what had come of it. A man had lost his life. Most of the children, including Caleb, who was Ben's cousin, had heard the gossip. They knew what Ben had done. But Seth didn't know about it yet. At least, she didn't think so. Maybe one of the other kids had told him. And how would that look once Seth found out? Ben had just told the boys not to fight, yet he was a hypocrite for killing a man.

And then a thought occurred to Caroline. It wasn't fair for her to hold a grudge against Ben because of his past. If she truly believed in the forgiveness of Jesus Christ, then who was she to keep remembering what he'd done? She understood that everyone could repent and all sins could be washed away and forgotten. The scriptures talked about sinful men casting stones at others, and she had her own failings to work on. And if that was the case, who better than Ben to help her soften Seth's anger?

Hmm. Maybe she should ask Ben what he thought.

Ben leaned against the buggy and folded his arms. Like many times before, he was waiting on a woman. Waiting for Caroline. But he didn't mind. After all, it was the task the bishop had assigned him. And he realized every time he was waiting on a woman, it was because she was serving someone else. How could he ever begrudge that?

An hour earlier he'd watched as she'd come outside to greet Sarah and Hannah when they'd picked up their kids from school. She'd spoken with both women about Caleb and Seth's fight today. Ben had kept his distance, busying himself with pouring cement to anchor the swing set into the ground. But he'd seen the surprise and then the revulsion on each woman's face when they found out their boys had been fighting at school. It was such a rare occurrence in an Amish school. But for one of the bishop's sons to be a participant must be a great embarrassment for Sarah. After all, the bishop's *familye* should set an example for everyone else in the *Gmay*. They should be above reproachful behavior. And Ben could just imagine the severe conversation he would hear later that evening at the supper table when his uncle addressed the issue with Caleb.

Now a soft scuffle caused him to turn. Caroline stood on the landing of the front steps, locking the door to the schoolhouse. Finally, she was ready to go home. But from the set of her shoulders and the way she inclined her head, he could tell she was still distraught.

He stepped near, just close enough to catch her should she stumble on the stairs. When he'd first been given this assignment, he'd learned really fast that she wanted to do things by herself, if she could. And he admired her spunk. In spite of great odds, she hadn't become clingy or whiney. She was as strong and independent as it was possible to be in her situation. But he wasn't sure he could help her with this new problem. It was way over his head.

"Danke," she said when he offered his arm for her to climb into the buggy.

It delighted him that she didn't push him away, and he realized she was coming to accept his presence at the school without objection.

With a nod, he hurried around to his side of the buggy and took the leather lead lines into his hands. They drove in silence for a short time, and he purposefully didn't intrude on her thoughts. He'd learned enough about this woman to know there were times when she needed to be left alone.

"Mary hasn't been sleeping very well since the funeral. Sometimes she has bad nightmares," she finally said.

Hmm. That was an interesting subject for her to bring up out of the blue.

"*Ach*, I'm not surprised. Losing their *eldre* can't have been easy on either her or Seth. Especially since they were there when the accident occurred. They may have witnessed some horrible things that haunt their memories," he said.

She glanced at him. "You're right. They were there and saw it all. *Ach*, the poor little lambs."

Her chin wobbled slightly and she lifted a hand to her face. Her fingers trembled and he thought she might cry. He hated to see her in distress and wanted to comfort her.

"Don't worry. As you and the rest of your *familye* show them a lot of love and support, they'll adjust soon enough. The entire *Gmay* will make those two *kinder* feel loved and wanted," he said, remembering exactly how it felt to lose his own parents. He'd adjusted to living without them but had never recovered from the loss. And he feared Mary and Seth might suffer the same fate.

One of the windows was open, and the ties to Caroline's white organdy prayer *kapp* waved in the breeze.

He longed to reach out and tug on it and tease a smile from her lips.

"How long did it take for you to get over losing your *eldre*?" she asked.

Here it was. The one question he didn't want to face. He stared straight ahead, concentrating on the road. Losing his parents when he was so young had devastated him. Not a day went by that he didn't miss them terribly.

"I'll let you know if I ever do," he said.

She heaved a deep sigh. "I'm afraid both Mary and Seth have taken their *eldre's* deaths quite hard. But even with the sleeplessness, Mary is still talkative and affectionate. She's folded right into our *familye* gatherings at home."

"*Ja*, I've noticed she seems to gravitate to you quite a bit," he said.

She nodded. "We have become quite close already. She's so easy to love. But Seth is another matter. I'm worried about him. He's so quiet and surly all the time. I've tried to get him to open up and talk but he won't say a word. He's so withdrawn, even with *Aent* Hannah and *Onkel* Mervin. And now he's picking fights at school. I asked him to draw a picture of how he was feeling and he wadded up the paper and threw it across the room. I'm not sure how to get through to him."

A blaze of delight speared Ben's chest. He couldn't believe Caroline was confiding all of this in him. It was the first time she'd purposefully started a conversation with him, as if she were seeking his advice.

"*Ach*, that was how he was feeling, then," he said.

"What do you mean?" she asked.

"He wadded up the paper and threw it away. That was his drawing. He didn't need a pencil or crayon to show you what he felt inside, just his hands to wad up the paper."

A look of amazement covered her face, as if a light had clicked on inside her mind. "*Ach!* I see what you mean. I didn't think to look at it that way. I'll talk to him about it when I get *heemet* tonight. You're absolutely right. The wadded-up paper was his artwork. But I need to ask him about the pocketknife, too. If it's going to be a problem, I don't want him to bring it to school again."

"*Gut* idea. Seth is tall and husky for his age, so he's kind of a target for older boys, just like I was at his age," Ben said.

Caroline snorted. "Caleb is quite a bit older than Seth and has been known to cause mischief before, but I don't think he picked the fight today."

"I agree," Ben said. "I don't know all the details, but Seth has suffered a great loss recently. He's angry and hurting and doesn't know where he belongs in the world. That can make him want to lash out at others for no real reason."

"*Ach*, he belongs here with us, of course. I don't know why he doesn't get that," she said, not seeming to understand.

They pulled onto the county road and he took a moment to consider his words carefully before he responded. "Of course he belongs here but he doesn't quite know that yet. He's filled with a great deal of anger and doesn't know how to control it right now."

She glanced at him. "You seem to have some things

in common with Seth. Maybe…maybe you could speak with him?"

It was a question, not a statement. He couldn't believe she was actually asking for his help.

"*Ja*, I'd be happy to talk to him. But I can't tell you how much I regret what happened to me. I don't want Seth to ever go through that. Not ever."

Another long pause.

"He'll probably hear about it sooner or later," she said.

"*Ja*, I should tell him first and explain that violence isn't the way to go. It brings nothing but pain and discouragement," he said.

"What did happen to you?" she asked.

He inhaled sharply. No one had ever asked him to talk about it, not even his two uncles. Only the police had asked for his side of the story, and he hadn't discussed it with anyone else since that terrible time many years earlier.

"I… I lost both my parents when I was young, and as I mentioned, I was large for my age, just like Seth." He spoke in an aching whisper, the memories washing over him in shattering waves. "I was always peaceful inside, but I became a target of some older *Englisch* boys who wanted to fight because I was so tall. They'd been dogging me around town for months, even coming out to my *onkel's* fields when I was there working alone. I was able to avoid trouble for quite some time. But one day they caught me alone in an alleyway in town."

His heart pounded in his chest and he gripped the lead lines harder. He felt like it had just occurred, and he wasn't sure he wanted to talk about this anymore.

"What happened?" she pressed.

He took a deep inhale, trying to steady his nerves. "They knew the Amish didn't fight and they took delight in goading me. I... I was only seventeen at the time. Too young to know my own strength and too young to have the self-confidence I needed to resist them. There were nine of them. I took their beating without so much as a murmur, until one of them started calling my *mudder* foul names. Then I... I lost it."

Even now, after years of being without his mother, the pain still felt fresh. His dear, sweet mother. So gentle, kind and good. The one person in this world who had loved him unconditionally. He couldn't stand the thought of anyone besmirching her pure name. And something had happened inside him that day that he still didn't understand. A fury had washed over him like he'd never felt before. It had boiled up inside him like a raging inferno, completely out of control. But he didn't tell Caroline that.

"I didn't strike anyone with my fists. I never lashed out. But when one of the young men got in my face and called my *mudder* names, I pushed him away," he continued. "He fell back and hit his head on the edge of the cement gutter. I tried to help him but he died in my arms."

She gasped. "Oh, Ben! I'm so sorry for what you've been through, but you must know it was wrong for you to use any force whatsoever, even to push someone away. If you hadn't pushed that man, he wouldn't have fallen and struck his head. He wouldn't have died."

He nodded. "*Ja*, I know better than anyone how tragic it can be to fight back. And oh, how I wish I hadn't. I might have been the one to die that day, but that would have been preferable to being responsible for someone else's death."

Yes, he knew only too well how horrible it could be to use force. What had followed had been more than traumatic for him. Before the incident, he'd had many friends and numerous options for marrying a nice Amish girl. He'd had a bright future with his people. He was one of them and welcome in their homes.

But after what happened, they'd all turned away. Because he hadn't yet been baptized into the Amish faith, he hadn't been shunned, but he might as well have been. He'd killed a man and they wanted nothing to do with him. When he was in their homes, an uncomfortable silence prevailed. No one sought him out or spoke to him during church meetings, unless they needed him to help with a work project. He didn't belong with them anymore. He didn't belong anywhere.

"What happened after you…after you…?" She didn't finish her question but she didn't need to.

He took a deep breath, thinking maybe it was good to get the whole story out. To tell someone what really happened. But as he did so, he realized he was placing a lethal weapon in Caroline's hands. If she chose, she could use the information to hurt him even more. By confiding in her, he was placing a lot of trust in her.

"Since nine men had attacked me, the law ruled it as self-defense," he said. "But I couldn't go anywhere alone anymore. Because they blamed me for killing one of their friends, the gang of *Englisch* boys increased their attacks on me. And during the months that followed, I learned firsthand about the pains of ostracism, loneliness and guilt. People in the *Gmay* turned their backs whenever I was near. They may not have formally shunned me, but I knew they wanted nothing to do with me. Finally, my *onkel* Amos invited me to come here to Riverton, to start afresh. He thought if he could get me out of that community, I could begin anew. But I don't think that's possible anymore. The gossip has followed me. Everyone in our *Gmay* knows what happened and no one wants me here, either."

She listened quietly but didn't say a word for a long time. She seemed to be digesting everything he'd told her and making her own judgments. Then she looked straight at him, unblinking.

"That's not true. The people in our *Gmay* want you, Ben. I think they're just getting to know you. But the people in your old community shouldn't have pushed you away. They should have shown you an increase of love and been more supportive," she said.

Her words shocked him. How kind and generous of her. And yet, he'd felt her disapproval, too. At first.

"I don't want Seth to go through what happened to you," she said. "I want him to grow up feeling loved and wanted. I want him to be happy. Will you help him, Ben? Please!"

Ben! He loved it when she said his name. It was an acknowledgment that he existed and was worthy of being part of her world.

"As you wish. I'll speak to him and try to make him understand that violence isn't how *Gott* wants us to live our lives. I'll talk with him about being passive and showing the same love for everyone that the Savior showed to us, even if it's someone who wants to harm us," he said.

"*Ach*, would you? I really think it might help. Especially since he looks up to you already. He really admires you," she said.

And that concerned him. Seth admired him, but once he found out what he had done, Ben feared the boy would be disappointed in him.

Caroline lifted a hand to touch Ben's, and he felt a surge of energy shoot up his arm. The gesture softened his heart. It made him feel confident. Like he would do anything for her. But then she jerked her hand away, as if she realized what she'd done and that she didn't want to touch him after all.

"Of course I'll do it. But I don't think he looks up to me. I think he's just a very lost little boy right now," he said, feeling pleased by her words but unable to really believe them.

"He does look up to you, Ben. Haven't you noticed how he watches you all the time when you're working in the schoolyard on the new playground equipment? And he stays close by you at church whenever you're around. *Aent* Hannah told him you'd lost your parents when you were young, and I think he feels a kinship with you because of it."

Ben blinked. "She did? He does?"

She laughed, the sound high and sweet and like honey to his heart.

"*Ja*, he does. You should pay more attention to him. Because he sure notices you," she said.

He smiled, too, and glanced her way. "I'll do just that. I'll shower him with attention."

Chapter Nine

This was a mistake. The moment Caroline suggested she make a picnic and go fishing with Ben and the two orphans, she regretted it. It had seemed like a good idea at the time, and she'd gotten caught up in making plans. But now she wasn't so sure. She had sympathy for Ben and the tragic events that had brought him here to Riverton, but she also wasn't sure she should spend extra time with him. What might people say? She didn't want them to think she and Ben were romantically involved. Because they weren't. They never would be. But now it was too late to back out.

As promised, Ben picked her and the children up on Saturday, just after they'd finished their morning chores. She'd spent a lot of extra time talking and reading to both Seth and Mary each evening. And when she'd asked Seth about the pocketknife he'd brought to school, she'd been shocked to find out it had belonged to his father. When he'd accidentally dropped it on the playground at school and Caleb Yoder had picked it up, Seth had gone ballistic and attacked the other boy. For some reason Seth had felt threatened, even though Caleb was trying to return the knife and meant no harm. Now Seth felt horrible for what he'd done.

Aunt Hannah was relieved that Caroline had taken such an active role in Seth and Mary's discipline. She was too busy with her own brood and didn't know how to handle a rebellious boy like Seth. The situation was foreign to her, and she was happy to abdicate her parenting role.

Though the farmers expected a killing frost any day now, even the late-October weather wouldn't cancel their fishing trip. The sun was shining bright, not a cloud in the sky. In fact, the warm day felt more like summer than fall.

"Is this all you're taking with you?" Ben asked.

Standing at the back door, he hefted the large wicker basket where Caroline had stowed their picnic lunch—ham and cheese sandwiches, deep-dish apple pie and ruffled potato chips bought yesterday from the grocery store in town. It would be an extra special treat the children should enjoy since they didn't get them very often.

"And that, too, please." Caroline pointed at a folded blanket she'd laid on the kitchen table.

"I wanna go fishing, too." Five-year-old Benuel sat at the table finishing his breakfast of eggs and toast.

Aunt Hannah turned from the stove. "Remember we talked about this? Ben and Caroline are taking just Mary and Seth this morning. Your *daed* will take you into town with him once his chores are done."

The boy scowled and stirred his fork around in his eggs. Eight-year-old Joseph and ten-year-old Levi frowned from their seats nearby, too. Caroline knew her aunt had explained the situation to her children, but they still weren't happy to be excluded. After all, most Amish children enjoyed fishing. It was a chance to escape the constant drudgery of work and do something fun. But Caroline feared that, if they took the other children along, Seth and Mary might get lost in the shuffle. Caroline's aunt and uncle had agreed that the orphans needed a special day all to themselves.

Besides, Hannah had been all smiles ever since Caroline informed her of Ben's idea to spend extra time with Mary and Seth. No doubt Hannah hoped the outing would draw Caroline and Ben closer, too. And while Caroline didn't disabuse her aunt of such notions, she had no intention of letting that happen.

It was becoming more and more difficult not to like Ben, especially after all that he'd told her. She understood how bad he felt for causing the death of that young man. And she thought Ben had repented of his actions. He deserved the right to move past it all. But that didn't mean they were anything more than friends. Because there were other barriers between them, such as the fact that she could never have a child of her own.

Ben gathered up the blanket, then turned with the basket and went outside to stow the items in the back of the buggy. The screen door clapped closed behind him. Mary and Seth were already outside. From the open doorway, Caroline could see Mary hopping around with excitement. But Seth just stood beside the horse, his head hanging as he kicked at a stone with the tip of his black boot.

"*Ach*, I guess I better get out there," Caroline said.

Hannah stepped over and hugged her tight. "Have

fun, dear. And be sure to laugh at least twice today. This is such a *gut* idea. Seth and Mary aren't the only ones who need a nice outing. I think you and Ben need it, too."

Caroline froze. She wasn't sure that was true, but it didn't matter anymore. Bracing her cane in front of her, she walked out into the brilliant sunshine.

"*Komm* on, Seth. It's time to go," Ben called to the boy as he helped first Mary and then Caroline into the buggy.

The boy did as he was told and sat in the back with his sister. Within minutes Ben directed the horse onto the county road, but they only traveled on it for a quarter of a mile before he turned off again.

"Where are we going?" Mary leaned forward and rested her chin on Ben's shoulder as she looked out the windshield.

"Over to Cherry Creek. I know a nice little spot where we can catch some fine trout," he said.

"I don't wanna go fishing," Seth grumbled from the backseat.

"*Ach*, then you can sit in the buggy while we go fishing. But I suspect that will get pretty boring after a while," Ben responded with a heavy dose of laughter in his voice.

Though he was teasing the boy, Caroline swiveled in her seat and saw that Seth was wearing a grumpy frown. The child wasn't amused, and she wished he would climb out of his doldrums.

They soon arrived at their destination, a sparkling pond of water along Cherry Creek where beams of golden sunlight shimmered against the pebbled shore.

Ben parked the horse and buggy beneath the shade of tall aspens. Before doing anything else, he helped everyone out of the buggy, then offered the horse a drink and let the animal nibble at the tall sedge grass.

Caroline helped retrieve the fishing box from the back of the buggy, then chose a grassy spot near the shore to spread out the blanket. Mary was off like a shot, racing down to the water's edge.

"Not too far, *liebchen*. Stay where I can see you at all times," Caroline called to the girl.

"I will," Mary responded in a happy voice. She picked up a stick and poked the ground, turning over rocks and studying bugs in the dirt.

Smiling with satisfaction, Caroline sat down, thinking this was a perfect vantage point for her to watch the children fish with Ben. Tall sedges and cattails grew along the embankment, the water crystal clear and rippling like liquid glass. It was absolutely lovely here.

"I didn't know the bishop had such a beautiful fishing hole on his property," she told Ben.

He shook his head and set the wicker basket beside her on the blanket. "This land doesn't belong to my *onkel*. It's part of my land."

She blinked. "Your land?"

"*Ja*, I own thirty acres bordering my *onkel's* property. I bought it from him a year ago but haven't had time to clear and plant the land yet."

Really! She'd had no idea Ben had bought farmland here in the Riverton area. She just assumed he would live out his entire life working on the bishop's farm.

"What will you grow here?" she asked.

He gazed at the open fields of land spreading out before them. And in her mind's eye, she could just imagine fences and furrows he would build one day.

"Mostly hay and a little barley and oats. I doubt I can grow much of anything else," he said.

She nodded. "*Ja*, it's too cold here in this valley. Before my accident, I always covered our tomato plants at night and got a nice harvest that way. My *aent* and I bottle a lot of produce from our garden. We Amish do okay here in Colorado. And it's a *wundervoll* place to raise a *familye*."

The moment she said that, she regretted it. She didn't want to give him the wrong idea. They could never be more than friends and even that was iffy. But she realized the more time they spent together, the more friendly they had become.

"I plan to raise horses, too. This is a great place for our Amish people to live. We have wide open spaces for our farms and can practice our faith without anyone bothering us," he said.

"This is near the Harlin place, isn't it?" she asked, trying to change the subject.

He nodded. "*Ja*, the house is right over there."

He jutted his chin toward an open field that was overgrown by tall weeds and wild grass. Off in the distance, Caroline could just make out the shapes of a white farmhouse and tall, red barn. And all at once, the ramifications of her cousins' deaths washed over her like a cold dunk in the river. Anna and James weren't here to buy the place. They'd never get to live in the farmhouse or raise hay and livestock. Little Mary and Seth would never grow up here. All their dreams had been dashed to pieces.

Caroline looked away and blinked fast so Ben and the children wouldn't see the sudden tears that filled her eyes. She wondered what would happen to the Harlin farm now that James and Anna were gone. Already the place had been neglected. An outlying farm like this didn't sell fast here in Colorado. It was too remote from the town. Also, with the short growing season, colder weather and drought issues, it was hard work to make a go of such a place. No doubt the years would take their toll and the farm would fall into disrepair and ruin. It was so sad, really. A home like that was meant to be lived in. Caroline had always dreamt of occupying just such a farm with her husband one day. Instead, she must be happy staying with her aunt and uncle on their place.

Ben handed a fishing pole to Seth but the boy just stared at it. No doubt he understood their brief conversation and was missing his parents, too.

"Did you ever go fishing with your *vadder*?" Ben asked as he opened a container of night crawlers.

"*Ja*, of course I did," Seth said, his voice defensive.

"*Gut!* Then you know how to bait a hook."

Seth frowned with uncertainty.

"Yuck! I'm not gonna bait a hook," Mary said from nearby.

Ben chuckled. "Don't worry. You won't have to. Not as long as we men are here to do it for you." He turned and faced Seth again. "I'm glad you have some *gut* memories with your *vadder*, Seth. He'll always be your *daed* and no one can ever take those memories away from you."

The boy stared as Ben turned and headed toward the water. Not seeming to know what else to do, Seth followed. Caroline watched as the two sat together on a large boulder, their fishing poles lying beside them as they baited their hooks. From what she could tell, they didn't speak much. And in spite of his words, Seth didn't seem to know what to do. With utmost patience, Ben showed him how to bait the hook and then cast out his line.

Mary picked up some rocks and tried to skim them across the surface of the pond. Instead, they raised great geysers as the stones pounded the water. Caroline longed to join her, but the rocky shore was so uneven that she feared she might fall.

"*Schtopp* throwing rocks, Mary! You'll scare all the fish away," Seth snapped.

Mary frowned and came walking back to Caroline, her slender shoulders slumped in discouragement. The girl plopped down on the blanket beside her and released a giant huff.

"Fishing isn't so much fun for a girl," she said.

Oh, no! This outing had to be fun for both children. What could she do to make Mary happy today?

"You can fish, too, if you want to. Ben would let you hold his pole. Why don't you go and ask him?" Caroline suggested.

"But I don't want to catch the poor little fish. I'd only want to throw them back. I'm bored," Mary said.

Kneeling on the blanket, Caroline reached to clasp a tree trunk and pulled herself up. Though she still needed help, it was definitely getting easier. "*Ach*, we can't have that. How about if you and I go look for some pretty pinecones to take home with us? I promised *Aent*

Hannah I'd make a wreath for Christmas this year. You can help me gather them up. Okay?"

Caroline held out her hand, and the girl immediately smiled and clasped her fingers as she hopped to her feet.

Though she had to move slowly, Caroline found the soft leaf litter and needles much easier to walk on than the pebbled beach. She moved through the surrounding trees, searching for some pine trees. Mary smiled happily and, when they found some particularly pretty cones, she eagerly gathered them into a brown paper bag Caroline supplied.

Soon, they both got hungry and headed back to shore. They returned at just the right time. Seth's fishing line gave a hard tug and his reel began to buzz. Taken off guard, the boy almost dropped the fishing pole into the pond. Ben grabbed the handle and pulled backward before he placed the rod in Seth's smaller hands.

"Don't let go, Seth. Reel him in," Ben encouraged, helping him.

Mary squealed with delight and ran over to cheer her brother on. "Pull him in, Seth. Pull him in."

Together, Ben and Seth alternatively tugged and reeled until the eight-inch trout was safely on the shore. Ben helped the boy snag the thrashing fish with the net. Once the catch was secure, Caroline saw something she never thought possible. Seth grinned wide and held the fish up high.

"Look, Mary! I caught one! I actually caught my first fish," the boy crowed.

He laughed out loud, and Caroline could only stare at him in wonder. It was the first time she'd heard such a happy sound come from the boy, and it surprised her. Then she remembered what Aunt Hannah had told her—to make sure she laughed at least twice today. And with that thought rippling through her mind, Caroline did just that.

Hearing her enjoyment, Ben glanced her way, looking both pleased and startled by the sound. He laughed, too, and Caroline realized she couldn't remember the last time she'd had so much fun.

Regaining her composure, she hugged Seth and congratulated him over and over again. Within minutes he had his hook baited and was perched on the boulder, ready to snag another one.

"I don't want to disappoint Hannah, so I better catch some more fish for supper tonight," Seth said, his expression intense and his voice filled with delight.

Mary sat beside her brother, chatting away about how beautiful his little trout was and how tasty she knew it would be once they ate it later that evening. The two children looked incredibly happy, and Caroline realized their outing had been a great success.

Ben turned and looked at Caroline from over his shoulder. His eyes twinkled with merriment as he pushed his black felt hat back on his head. Then he did something that both startled and delighted her. He winked and mouthed one single word to her.

Victory!

Caroline nodded and looked away, unable to contain a smile of satisfaction. Yes, she couldn't agree more. They'd had a great triumph today. Hearing Seth's laughter and seeing him so animated and excited had made this trip worth the effort. Both children were happy. So was Caroline. And for a short time, she'd been able to pretend that this was her *familye*. That the children belonged to her. But soon, they would go home. They would have to return to reality. Because these weren't her kids, and Ben would never be her husband. No, not in a million years.

"How come you don't fish, Teacher Caroline?" Mary asked sometime later when they were eating their lunch.

Ben listened, eager to hear Caroline's response. She had just taken a bite of sandwich and chewed, then swallowed before answering.

"I used to fish, when I was younger. In fact, I'd go with your *mamm* and *daed* and we'd have a nice picnic lunch just like we're eating today," she said.

"You did?" Seth's forehead furrowed in a disbelieving frown.

She nodded. "*Ja*, remember your *mudder* is my first cousin once removed and I've known both your *eldre* all my life. Your *mamm* was five years older than I am but we grew up together back when I lived in Ohio. Because I was younger, she always looked after me like a big sister."

"Really?" Mary asked.

Caroline nodded and Ben liked the sweet way she spoke to the children.

"Really. My grandmother and your *mamm's* mother were sisters. So you see? We really are *familye*. And I have lots of memories of your *eldre*."

"What memories?" Seth asked.

Caroline smoothed her black skirt for a moment, as if she were thinking back to the days when she'd been young.

"I remember going to church with your *mamm*. She made the best apple strudel I've ever eaten. Because my *mudder* died when I was sixteen, Anna came to stay at my *vadder's* house for a few weeks, to cook and clean and help take care of my younger *bruder* and *schweschder*. She was so sweet and made me feel like everything was going to be all right. Now I hope I can repay the favor by helping you feel happy and realize that you're both going to be okay."

She hugged Mary, and the girl snuggled against her side, accepting her words without reservation. But Seth gazed at her, his expression one of deep thought.

"Can you tell us about our *vadder*?" Mary asked.

"Of course. I always looked up to James. He was seven years older than I am, and I thought he was so strong and handsome. All the girls in the *Gmay* were crazy about him, but he only had eyes for your *mudder*. He would pick wildflowers for Anna, and all the other boys would tease him about it. But he didn't care one bit," Caroline said.

"*Ja*, our *daed* loved our *mamm*," Mary said, nodding.

"He sure did, and your *mamm* adored your *vadder*. Your *mamm* taught me how to crochet," Caroline said.

"She did?" Mary asked with awe.

Caroline nodded. "She was much better at it than I am. Her stitches were so small and even. And your *vadder* was always the fastest boy on the playground. No one could beat him in a footrace. But he was kind, too. I remember once one of the other *kinder* came to school without their lunch, and he shared his with them without even being asked."

Ben listened as Caroline related story after story

about the children's parents. The kids seemed enthralled as they absorbed every word. Likewise, Ben enjoyed hearing about Caroline's childhood. Finally, when it was time to go home, they packed up the wicker basket, the fishing poles and fish, and loaded them into the buggy. It was late afternoon and they'd had a marvelous day. Ben was sad to see it end.

As the horse trotted down the county road, the comfortable swaying of the buggy soon lulled the two children to sleep. With them in the back and Caroline sitting next to him in the front, Ben got a sense of peace he hadn't felt in a long time. It was as if this was how it should be. All of them together like one happy *familye*. But he had to remind himself that these weren't his kids and Caroline wasn't his wife. And from what she'd told him, she never would be.

"They had a *gut* day." Caroline spoke softly enough that she didn't awaken the kids.

"*Ja*, I did, too. *Danke* for this outing," he said, unable to remember enjoying a better time in his life.

"Do you think it will help with Seth's fighting at school?" she asked.

He shrugged. "Who knows? It couldn't hurt. But no matter what, we've created some happy memories for the two kids."

She smiled, her expression soft and easy. And once again, he thought he'd never seen a more beautiful woman in all his life.

"You seemed to know just what to say and how to help the kids today," she said.

"And you also. Telling the *kinder* so many stories about their *eldre* was just what they needed. I'm sure it helped them feel closer to their *mamm* and *daed*. And I'm sure it helped them feel closer to you, too."

She looked down at her hands, which were folded in her lap. "I hope so. Have you had the opportunity to speak with Seth about fighting yet?"

"*Ja*, I reminded him that his *vadder* is counting on him to be a *gut* boy and watch out for his little sister. That's what I talked to him about while we were fishing. I encouraged him not to let his *daed* down by fighting. I told him I knew firsthand how bad it could be, but I didn't lay it on too thick. I didn't want to spoil the day with such a heavy topic. But I'll address the issue again as time goes on," he said.

"You're wise. I doubt this problem will be fixed with just one outing. It'll take a bit of time," she said.

"*Ja*, it may take a lifetime of love and support. But we can provide it. As long as we don't give up on these two *kinder*, they'll know we're always here for them and they'll both come around soon enough."

"I agree. They need consistency and love. That's all any of us needs," she said.

He nodded, wishing they could be so much more than friends. But deep in his heart, he knew he must not expect anything else. Because he could never meet her expectations.

"What do you suppose will happen to the Harlin place now that James and Anna aren't here to buy it?" she asked.

He shrugged. "It'll sit empty, I suppose. And one day, years from now, some *familye* will buy the land and make a go of it."

He wished he could buy the place. It bordered the

property he'd recently bought from his uncle, so it would be perfect for him. With the added acreage, he would have plenty of land to farm. He could raise hay and livestock to sell. And the house and barn were already built. All he would have to do was tidy up the house, move in and go to work. But what good would it do for him to live in a big old farmhouse by himself? A place like that needed a wife and children to make it complete. He couldn't stand the thought of moving in and becoming an old Amish bachelor there. That kind of loneliness would break his heart.

They didn't speak much after that. No doubt they were both lost in their own thoughts and regrets. And just like Seth, Ben was determined to hold on to his good memories. To be a credit to his mother and father. Because once Caroline no longer needed his help at the school, he would need his sweet memories of her to sustain him through the long, lonely days to come.

Chapter Ten

A week later Caroline stood outside in the schoolyard and gazed at the white flower boxes Ben had installed beneath each windowsill. It was the first of November, and the weather had caused a distinct chill in the air, even though the afternoon sun gleamed bright against the autumn leaves and the slight breeze made the flowers tremble slightly. Because the boxes were tucked close to the schoolhouse, the pansies had clung to the warmth and remained bright and colorful. But Caroline knew a killing frost would soon end that.

Turning, she gazed at the children as they played a game of baseball. Their happy chatter and laughter filled the air. Recess didn't last long, and they were eager to make the best of it. They'd gobbled down their lunches, then picked up where they'd left off the last time they played. They didn't pick sides but simply rotated positions and ensured everyone had a turn at batting. It was so pleasant to see Seth getting along well with Caleb Yoder. Maybe they were through the worst of it, and Seth was beginning to adjust to his new life.

Though they never kept score, the kids were highly competitive and did their best. Just now, the bases were loaded as little Leron Albrecht came up to bat. Though the boy was merely five years old, his solid stance and intense expression told Caroline that he was determined to hit the ball and bring the runners home.

But where were Mary and Seth?

Leaning heavily on her cane, Caroline turned, her gaze scanning the schoolyard. Walking toward the baseball diamond, she noticed Ben was missing, too. Normally, he stood on the sidelines, yelling encouragement to the batter or correcting their stance. But he wasn't there today.

Several nights ago Aunt Hannah had presented her with a thin, wooden cane. Caroline had been more than happy to cast aside the elbow crutch. She'd been a bit wobbly at first. But now she could move more easily on her own and hadn't fallen in over a week. Soon she planned to get rid of the cane, too.

She turned and scanned the area for some sign of the missing man and children. She saw them, sitting near the embankment where Cherry Creek ran through the middle of Bishop Yoder's property. Ben sat on a tree stump with little Mary on his knee. She had her arm draped around the big man's shoulders. Seth stood beside them holding a stick and was scraping the pointed end against the ground.

She could tell Ben was speaking. Now and then, Seth would nod in acquiescence. Both children seemed to be listening intently, and Caroline wished she could overhear their conversation. It appeared that Ben was keeping his word and continuing to work with Seth. He was showing an increase of love for both kids and helping them realize they weren't alone. During school time and each night at home, Caroline tried to do the same.

Huddled together with their backs to Caroline, the three of them looked so lost and isolated from the other children. They each seemed adrift in a world they didn't know how to navigate. And a feeling of deep sorrow swept over Caroline. She understood all too well how they must feel. She wished she could make the children happy. How she longed to ease their loss—and more than anything to be their mom.

"Teacher Caroline! *Komm* and play with us."

Annie Beiler waved at her from the outfield. The kids had noticed she was getting around better, though she still didn't think she was up to hitting the ball and running the bases.

She smiled, waved and headed their way, but not before she saw that Ben and the two orphans had ended their discussion and were headed in her direction. Caroline waited for Ben to join her. Mary took up a position with Alice at third base while Seth went to replace Timmy Hostetler as catcher so Timmy could have a chance to bat.

"Are you going to play?" Ben asked.

Standing beside her, he slid his thumbs through his black suspenders. He'd removed his black felt hat when he'd been installing the rope to the new tether ball pole. Sunlight shimmered against his dark hair, and his eyes gleamed with merriment.

"*Ne*, I'm not up to it yet. But now that I'm using just this cane to walk, I feel more and more like my old self," she said.

He flashed a smile that crinkled his eyes. "*Ja*, you're getting around quite well. I've finished putting together all the new playground equipment. Soon, you won't need my help here at the school anymore."

She looked away, thinking how she'd become so used to his presence that she would miss him when he was gone. Of course, she wasn't going to admit that out loud. But over the past few weeks, her heart had softened toward Ben, and she realized he was a good friend and she'd come to like him very much. But knowing she could never give him children made her more resolved than ever to remain detached.

She took a step toward the schoolhouse, thinking it was almost time to ring the bell and call the children back to the classroom for lessons.

"I noticed you were talking to Mary and Seth," she said.

"*Ja*, they asked me if they'd ever see their *mudder* and *vadder* again."

She hesitated and glanced at his face. "And what did you tell them?"

"I told them *ja*, they would see their *eldre* again in heaven." He nodded with finality, as if that settled the matter.

"And what about Seth's fighting? Did that topic come up again?" More than anything, she hoped Seth's anger might dissipate and he'd be less confrontational with the other children.

"*Ja*, I told him of some calming techniques I use whenever I feel angry, sad or upset."

She continued to walk slowly toward the school. "And may I ask what those techniques are?"

He stopped and faced her. As she looked up into his eyes, she was surprised by his quiet expression. At that moment he showed no guile whatsoever. Just a kind thoughtfulness that touched her heart.

"I think of something that makes me happy. Something that brings me joy. I think about the future and all my hopes and dreams for what is yet to come, and it makes me feel better," he said.

She blinked, wondering what those happy things might be. Perhaps a wife and *familye* of his own? And working his farmland to build a future for them? She longed to ask but thought it was too personal to pry.

"And did Seth know of something that makes him happy?" she asked instead.

Ben inclined his head. "*Ja*, he thinks of fishing. His heart is still filled with hurt but I think he's getting better. I suggested a few other things, and both he and Mary realized they have a lot to be thankful for."

Hmm. Caroline had never thought about doing that before. Her mind scanned the myriad blessings in her life. People and things that brought her great joy. And she was startled to realize that Ben was one of those people who made her feel happy inside.

"*Danke* for speaking with Seth and Mary today. I'm sure it will make a difference for them," she said.

A loud cheer came from the baseball diamond. Leron had gotten a hit, and the shortstop made a pretense of dropping the ball so the little boy could make it to first base. Caroline laughed as everyone whooped and congratulated Leron. And she realized one of the things that made her happy was these children. Their goodness and kindness to one another.

"*Ach!* I better get inside and ring the school bell. I think we're way overdue to resume our lessons," she said.

Ben nodded. "You go ahead and take the *kinder* inside. Since you're short on time, I'll clean up the baseball equipment for them today."

"*Danke,*" she called over her shoulder as she hurried toward the front steps.

As she picked up the heavy hand bell and rang it several times, she watched Ben's long stride as he hurried over to the home plate. The kids came running, and he waved some of them on when they tried to pick up the two bats and ball.

Once the last child hurried through the door, she stepped inside. It was Seth, his face flushed from running. He hung back from the other children, but she noticed his eyes didn't seem as sullen and angry today. In fact, his shoulders were no longer tensed, either. Maybe Ben's words to the boy were having an impact. She sure hoped so.

As she went inside and closed the door, she couldn't help thinking what a difference Ben had made in her own life. He'd become a confidant of sorts. Someone she could confide in and ask for advice. He'd taken a lot of physical burdens off her shoulders, too. His kindness and generosity had made it possible for her to teach the children this year. But soon, he'd be gone. Because he was part of her *Gmay*, she would see him regularly at church and other gatherings, but it wouldn't be the same. And she knew, when he stopped coming to the schoolhouse, she was definitely going to miss his presence and their daily chats.

* * *

On the ride home that afternoon, Ben waited for Caroline to speak. Other than to discuss Seth and Mary, she'd never talked much to him, but she was even more quiet than usual. He wondered what was on her mind. Perhaps she was thinking about Seth and Mary or another student who was having trouble with their studies. He knew she loved each of the scholars and fretted over how to help them. Each one was unique, with their individual strengths and weaknesses. Her care reminded Ben that *Gott* must feel the same about His children.

"I think Seth has made a lot of progress just over the past few weeks since he came to live here," he said.

Caroline jerked, as if his voice had startled her out of her musings.

"*Ja*, he's at least trying to do his schoolwork now. I was worried that first week after they arrived. All he would do was stare off into space. He wouldn't even make an effort," she said.

As they skirted the dirt road, Ben gazed at the thick stand of shrub oaks lining the bishop's outer field. Higher up in the Wet Mountains, he could see tall stands of aspen shimmering in the sunshine. The fall weather had brought cooler temperatures at night and the leaves had fallen, revealing the barren, jagged branches of tree limbs.

They rode in silence for a short time. A gust of chilly wind buffeted the buggy. Caroline shivered and he reached back for the blanket he kept on the backseat and handed it to her.

"*Danke*," she said as she spread the warm folds over her legs.

He glanced at her cane. "That must give you a lot more freedom."

"It does. I'll soon be walking on my own."

"I'm glad," he said.

She smiled with satisfaction, and he was truly happy for her. It had been a long, grueling recovery. At one point no one believed she'd ever walk again. But with her determination and tenacity, she'd beaten the odds. And though *Hochmut*, the pride of men, was something his people shunned, Ben couldn't help feeling proud of her accomplishment. But he didn't tell Caroline that. Nor did he tell her that, when he was feeling down, he thought about her to make him happy again.

The blare of a horn startled him and he looked into his rearview mirror. A black pickup truck had pulled up right behind them, hugging their rear bumper way too close. Ben knew exactly who the driver was.

Rand Henbury.

Caroline gasped and pressed a hand against the wall of the buggy as she swiveled around in her seat to get a better look. When she saw who it was, she made a small sound of anguish in the back of her throat. Her face drained of color, her eyes opening wide.

"Oh, *ne*!" she cried.

Ben slowed the horse, pulling him over to the shoulder of the road to give Rand plenty of room to pass. But the truck stayed right on their tail. Rand blared his horn again and again. In confusion, the horse jerked sporadically, showing his distress.

"Can you pull all the way off and let him pass?" Caroline begged.

Ben did just that, pulling off onto a dirt road. To keep

from appearing confrontational, he waited to get out of the buggy, hoping Rand would zip on by. Raising his arm in a crude gesture, that was exactly what Rand did. Ben got out and soothed the agitated horse. And when he got back inside, he had to do the same for Caroline. She didn't speak, but he could see from her frightened expression that she was absolutely terrified.

He touched her arm. "It's *allrecht*, Caroline. He's gone now. You don't need to be afraid."

She breathed in short, panicked gasps as she met his gaze. "I… I guess now is a *gut* time for me to think of something that makes me happy."

He chuckled. "*Ja*, I suppose all of us can use that technique when we're upset."

She showed a tentative smile and he knew she was trying her best to regain control. He squeezed her arm to let her know he was here and that everything would be okay. She turned away and he removed his hand. Not knowing what else to do, he gave her a moment to calm herself.

Staring out the window, she spoke in an aching whisper, so soft that he almost didn't hear. "I wish Rand wouldn't do that. It…it reminds me of the day of the accident when…when that drunk driver hit my buggy from behind. It's like I'm reliving it all over again."

Ah, now he understood. And he should have realized how something like that could upset her. Seth and Mary weren't the only ones who had suffered a bad trauma in their lives.

"No matter what Rand does, I won't let him or anyone else hurt you. Not ever," Ben vowed.

She faced him, her gaze locked with his. "Would you fight with him, Ben? Would you push him away, too?"

Her words were so startling that all he could do was stare at her. He had no answer. In his heart, he told himself that he wouldn't fight back. Never again. But if Rand did something to hurt Caroline, what would he do? He couldn't stand to see her injured again. Would he use force to stop Rand or someone else from harming her? He wasn't sure.

"Caroline, I…"

Her lips were slightly parted and her breath had slowed. More than anything, he wanted to keep her safe. To win her trust. And before he knew what was happening, he leaned his head down and kissed her. Softly. Like the gentle caress of butterfly wings.

She didn't resist but pressed the palm of her hand lightly against his chest. In his arms, she felt warm and sweet, and her fragrance spiraled around him in a mist that he longed to become lost in. Then she pulled away and he let her go.

"I… I really need to go home," she said, her voice wobbling as she pressed her fingertips against her lips.

"Of course." He took the lead lines into his hands and urged the horse to turn around.

Why had he kissed her? What had he been thinking? And what would her aunt and uncle say if they found out? What would the bishop think? No doubt they'd all be pleased. But he knew that marrying this woman would mean he could never have the children he longed for. He could never have a *familye*. And he had to ask himself, if Caroline had no reservations about being his wife, would he still want her?

The answer was a resounding yes!

However, it didn't matter because Caroline had made it perfectly clear that she wasn't interested in him. And he had to accept that.

He glanced over at Caroline and noticed she sat stiffly in her seat, her spine straight, her shoulders set in a solid block that reminded him she wanted nothing to do with him. Caroline was so wonderful and good. She deserved so much more than a man like him.

They didn't speak the rest of the way to the turnoff leading to her aunt and uncle's farm. The buggy rattled as it moved along the dirt road. Ben's mind whirled with turmoil. He longed to say something that might ease his guilty conscience. Something to let her know he meant her no harm. To apologize for kissing her. But he realized he wasn't sorry. It might be the first and last time he ever got to hold her that close, and he wanted to cherish the moment, not regret it.

He pulled up in front of her house and hurried to climb out. Fearing she might go inside before he could apologize, he took her arm to help her down. She quickly pulled away, as if his fingers had burned her skin.

"Caroline, I'm sorry. I didn't mean to frighten you. I didn't mean to take advantage, either," he said.

Standing on her own feet, she gripped her cane and looked up into his eyes. "I know. I didn't mean anything by it, either. And there's no need to apologize. We're both grown adults. But I meant what I said when you were first assigned to help me at the school. There can never be anything between us, Ben. Not ever. And I don't want to mislead you into thinking that has changed. So how about if we just forget it ever happened. Okay?"

She gave him a wan smile before stepping away. He stood there and watched her limp up the cobbled walk path leading to her uncle's back porch. The click of her cane striking the stones filled his mind, and he longed to go after her. Longed to deny what she'd just said. He'd kissed her, but he was a man and she was a woman and they could make their own choices now. But how could he ever forget her? How could he return to normal life again?

She disappeared inside, closing the door firmly behind her. She didn't look back. She didn't even peer out the window at him. He knew because he stood there and watched to see if she would.

He walked around to the driver's seat of his buggy. The conveyance rocked slightly as he climbed inside. Urging the horse forward, he pulled out of the graveled driveway, his mind filled with thoughts of Caroline. He'd killed a man, and no good woman would ever want him now. But Caroline wasn't just anyone. She was the only woman he'd ever seriously considered making his own. No other woman could take her place. Not in his heart. Nothing had changed for him. He could never marry. Never know the joys of having a *familye* of his own. Never feel the confidence of holding a woman's undying devotion and love. And though he thought he had accepted it and gotten on with his life, he realized it still hurt more than he could stand.

Chapter Eleven

Caroline stepped up onto the wooden boardwalk and turned to face the general store. It had been a week since Ben had kissed her. Or she'd kissed him. Or both. She wasn't sure anymore. She only knew it should never have happened. Because now she was haunted by the memory.

"I shouldn't be very long. I just need a few school supplies, and my *aent* Hannah asked me to also pick up some sour cream and a couple other groceries," she said.

Ben stood beside her, having just driven her into town and accompanied her safely to the front door of the grocery store. She'd told her uncle that morning that she could drive herself into town, but he wouldn't hear of it. Not with Rand Henbury on the loose. And even though she was now walking without even the help of her cane, the bishop had told her he wouldn't release Ben from his assignment of assisting her and the school until after the Thanksgiving holiday in two more weeks.

"I'll just pop into the building supply store for a few minutes and be right back to pick you up," Ben said.

He turned and hopped off the boardwalk with athletic agility before climbing into the buggy. She watched as he pulled away, heading down Main Street. The drive into town had been rather wooden and formal. Even their discussions about Seth and Mary were a bit stilted. After the kiss they'd shared, she felt embarrassed and didn't know what to say to him anymore. For those few short moments, she'd forgotten herself. Forgotten that she'd lost her ability to have children and shouldn't encourage any man's attention. Especially a man like Ben Yoder, who longed for a *familye* of his own and had suffered enough pain to last a lifetime. He deserved more than she could ever give him.

Heaving a sigh of frustration, she turned and went inside the store. It would do no good to feel sorry for herself, and she was determined to get on with her life.

Within minutes she'd purchased two special slide rulers and a box of chalk, as well as the food items her aunt needed. Placing them inside the wicker basket she was carrying, she stepped outside. A chilling breeze whipped past and she shivered, pulling her black woolen cape tighter around her throat. The sky was filled with leaden clouds, and the first snow of the season was forecasted for tonight. But she'd be home safe long before then. The fall harvest was secure. Over the past couple of weeks, even Ben had been hurrying home after dropping her off from school to help his uncle with the heavy workload. Her uncle and the other men of the *Gmay* had gathered up their hay just in time. Winter was upon them.

She glanced up and down the street but caught no sign of Ben or his black buggy. Deciding that she could use the exercise, she headed along the sidewalks toward the building supply store. As she moved along, she took special delight that she walked without the aid of any devices whatsoever. Her legs and hips were strong again, and she felt so happy and free.

Turning the corner, she bumped into someone and immediately drew back.

"Excuse me," she murmured.

Conditioned to stay as far away from *Englischers* as possible, she ducked her head and moved aside. But she stole a quick glance at the young man. Within a matter of seconds, a hard lump formed in her throat and she went all cold and clammy inside.

"Well, lookie who we have here. Our little cripple Amish girl. Where are your crutches, Amish girl?" Rand Henbury stood in the middle of the sidewalk, a snide grin on his face.

She tried to brush past him but he blocked her path. A feeling of absolute panic swept over her with the force of a hurricane, but she fought it off. She was a mature woman and had no reason to cower before this man. Rand was just a big bully, and she mustn't let him intimidate her.

Drawing herself up straight, she looked him square in the eyes.

"Excuse me, please," she said, trying once more to get by him.

"What have you got in there?" he asked, tugging on her wicker basket.

She pulled it away from him. "I beg your pardon but that is none of your business."

He laughed. "Woo-hoo! You beg my pardon? It looks

like you've got a little extra spice in you for an Amish girl."

He'd backed her up against the outside wall to the feed and grain store and reached out to tug on the ties to her black traveling bonnet.

"Please, let me go," she begged.

"What's your hurry, little Amish girl?" He leaned close and planted an arm against the wall beside her head.

Feeling boxed in, she cringed and turned her face away. Tears of frustration and fear burned the backs of her eyes. A sensation of absolute helplessness caused her arms and legs to tremble. If he didn't let her go soon, she was going to lose it. And she didn't want to crumble at his feet or show any other weakness before this man. But neither would she use force to get away from him.

"Let her go."

A low voice came from behind Rand, like the rumbling of thunder off in the distance.

Rand turned and Caroline saw Ben standing there, his expression severe. He towered over the *Englisch* man like a great hulking giant. He looked strong and stern, like a man who knew how to handle himself.

"What's it to you, Amish man?" Rand sneered.

Without a word, Ben reached around and clasped Caroline's wrist before pulling her behind him in a protective gesture.

"The buggy is parked in the back. Go on," Ben ordered her.

A feeling of outrage bubbled up inside Caroline. Who did Ben think he was, bossing her around like she belonged to him? Yes, her religion taught her to obey the men in her life, but Ben wasn't her husband. He wasn't even a relative.

And for that matter, who did Rand Henbury think he was? Blocking her path and taunting her? She wanted to yell and scream at both men to leave her alone. But she sensed that now was not the time for such actions.

"Come with me. You must not fight," she spoke to Ben in *Deitsch*, knowing Rand wouldn't be able to understand her words.

"I'll be along shortly, once I know you're safe," Ben said, never once taking his eyes off Rand.

Rand tilted his head. "What's that silly gibberish you're using? What are you saying?"

Neither Caroline nor Ben answered him. She'd heard that Rand was about eighteen years old and had just graduated from high school last spring. She had hoped he would leave town to go to college, yet he'd stayed. But it didn't seem that he spent his time working on his rich father's ranch, either. She couldn't help thinking he was wasting his life.

Rand stepped forward, lifting his chin as he glared at Ben. "I heard you killed a man back east somewhere. Is that true, Amish man?"

Ben didn't respond, but Caroline saw his hands clench. His eyes narrowed and his expression looked so fierce that she feared he might strike Rand.

"Come on, Ben. Please! Leave him." She tugged on his arm, desperate to get him out of there—as desperate to protect him from using violence as he was to protect her from Rand's harassment.

He shook her off, pushing her toward the buggy. "I'll be along shortly. Go on, now."

Feeling completely exasperated by the situation, she heaved a sigh and hurried away. In the back parking lot behind the building supply store, there was a covered canopy and hitching post with a sign that read Buggy Parking Only. Ben's buggy was the only one there, and she climbed inside and closed the door. Huddling on the front seat, she gazed out the window and wished Ben would come soon.

She thought he'd changed. Since he'd been helping her at the school and she'd gotten to know him well, she thought he'd gotten over his anger issues and was passive in the face of oppression. But now she wasn't so sure. If he started fighting, he might get hurt. Or worse. He might hurt or even kill Rand Henbury. She'd thought Ben had been truly repentant and had a humble heart. Yet, she feared she was dead wrong about him. Because what she'd seen today told her that Ben still had a lot of anger simmering just below the surface.

Ben wasn't a young seventeen-year-old boy anymore. Now he was a fully grown man who had been baptized into their Amish faith. And Rand's father had a lot of wealth. If Ben used force against Rand, she feared the consequences. He'd be shunned by their people. Because it would be a second offense, he could even be turned out of the *Gmay* for good. He could end up in jail. She'd never get to see him again. Never be able to talk with him or enjoy his comforting presence in her life. And that frightened her most of all.

Ben waited until Caroline disappeared around the corner to the Amish buggy parking lot. He stood like a mountain, keeping Rand from following after her. He didn't know what he would do if Rand tried to get past him, and he prayed the *Englischer* used more common sense than to try to chase after her.

"Ah, what's the matter, Amish man? You're not scared of little old me, are you?" Rand heckled him.

Ben almost snorted. He knew what he was capable of. If it was a matter of sheer strength, he could have picked Rand up and tossed him into the street with very little effort at all. But no matter what, he must not use force. He must remain passive. Because Caroline was counting on him and he couldn't let her down. But he felt a rage rising up inside him that made him want to pound Rand into a pulp.

That's not what Gott or Caroline would want me to do.

The thought entered his mind like a soft whisper. So quiet and gentle that he almost ignored it. And yet, he couldn't.

Ever since he'd kissed her, Caroline had been giving him the cold shoulder. She'd been kind and understanding when he'd told her about his past, but she didn't want to get tied up with a man like him. He couldn't let her down. Couldn't disappoint her by fighting. Nor did he want Seth to hear that he'd reverted to his old ways. He'd told the boy about his past, and Seth understood how badly he regretted it. What message would it send if Ben started fighting again? Not a good one, that was for sure.

And just like that, Ben let go of his anger. His clenched hands relaxed and his tensed shoulders eased. He didn't want to fight anymore. He wanted forgiveness. To go on with his life in joy and happiness.

As he gazed at Rand Henbury, a gentle peace enveloped him. Instead of seeing Rand as a threat, he saw him as a misguided boy who was insecure in himself and felt like he had to bully other people to boost his own self-esteem. With added insight, Ben thought maybe Rand's actions were a cry for attention from his own father. But Ben knew there was nothing he must face in this life that couldn't be reconciled through the forgiveness of Jesus Christ. He didn't have to fight. Not now, not ever again.

Two of Rand's friends stepped out of the café across the street. When they saw what was happening, they came running. Like wolves scenting blood, they surrounded Ben, their faces contorted in angry sneers.

"What's going on?" one of them asked Rand.

"Ah, this Amish man thinks he's a tough guy," Rand said mockingly. Then, emboldened by the presence of his friends, he shoved Ben back against the railing. "You're not so tough, are you, Amish man? You're big but you're a pacifist. You can't fight back, can you? You're a coward."

A coward. No, Ben wasn't a coward at all. Because in that moment he knew what was coming and he was prepared to take the beating no matter what. Even if it cost him his life, he was determined not to fight back in the slightest. And Caroline and Seth would both know that he'd kept his faith. Nothing else mattered right now.

"Hey! What do you boys think you're doing?"

Byron Stott, the owner of the building supply store, stepped out onto the sidewalk. Wearing a dingy carpenter's apron, he gripped a hammer in his hand.

"Don't you interfere, Byron. This has nothing to do

with you," Rand said, pointing a warning finger at the older man.

"Ben's done nothing to you. You leave him alone." Byron lifted the hammer in warning as he stepped closer.

"That's right. I've already called the police and they're on their way." Berta Maupin, the owner of the general store, stepped around the corner carrying a long-handled broom. "You boys had better skedaddle before they get here or you're gonna wish you had. The Amish are peaceful and we're not letting you harass Ben."

Seeing the commotion, Cliff Packer came out of the post office and jogged over to them. Several other *Englisch* people Ben didn't know stopped as they walked by. He hated to draw a big crowd and was desperate to escape this situation.

"You go on, Ben. Get in your buggy and go on home. I know you can't fight, but we can. We'll hold Rand here until you can get a good head start," Byron said.

Ben stared at them all, feeling dumbstruck. The townsfolk were *Englisch*, but they were protecting him. He could hardly believe this was happening.

And then a thought struck him. *Gott* had provided him with an escape. He had sent some guardians here to protect him so he wouldn't suffer a beating or break the vows of his faith by using force.

Taking this unexpected gift at face value, Ben turned and sauntered away. He didn't need to be told twice.

When he reached the buggy and opened the door to the driver's seat, Caroline jerked and whirled on him, her eyes filled with fear and tears.

Ah, did she have to cry? He hated that more than anything.

"Are you…are you okay?" she asked, her voice trembling.

"I'm fine."

Taking the lead lines into his hands, he directed the horse onto the road and hurried the animal into a fast trot out of town. He figured he had only minutes before Rand got away from the townsfolk and came after them in his black pickup truck.

"Did you…did you fight with Rand?" Caroline asked.

"*Ne*, I did not."

He didn't look at her, intent on getting her home now while he had the chance. There was safety in numbers, and he'd be sure to bring another man with him next time he came into town. The abuse from Rand and his cronies was escalating, and he didn't dare come alone from now on. Not if it meant Caroline might be hurt.

"I could see the anger in you. You still haven't overcome your violent tendencies," she said, her voice filled with accusation.

What could he say to that?

"I didn't hit him," he said.

"But you wanted to."

"I did, I won't deny it. At first. But I know *Gott* wouldn't approve. And neither would you. Being obedient to *Gott's* will doesn't always mean that we want to obey, but that we hand our will over to Him."

She nodded. "True, but obedience also requires that *Gott's* will becomes our own. And I don't think that's how you feel when it comes to anger."

Hmm, maybe she was right. But maybe it wasn't that simple, either.

"I have let go of my anger," he said. "I don't want to fight anymore, Caroline. I'd rather die first. And I was prepared to do just that today, if it meant you could leave and be safe."

Her mouth dropped open in surprise. But he meant what he'd said. Every single word. And he realized that, whether she believed in him or not, he believed in himself. He trusted *Gott*. And with the Lord beside him, he was never alone. Not even in his darkest moments. And knowing that, he realized *Gott* had forgiven him for what he'd done. Ben hadn't meant to kill anyone all those years earlier. He'd just been trying to get away from a crowd of thugs who wanted to beat him up. And in so doing, he'd caused one of their deaths. But now he wanted to go on living. To be happy and useful to others.

He wanted Caroline.

They were quiet for some time after that, with each of them lost in their own thoughts. And finally, Ben got the courage to ask Caroline a question that had been troubling him for months now.

"My *onkel* Amos told me that, after your buggy accident, you can't have children anymore. Is that true?" he asked.

Her head snapped around and she blinked at him with absolute shock. Then she turned and stared straight ahead. Her spine was ramrod straight, her delicate hands folded tightly in her lap. Ah, maybe he shouldn't have asked. It wasn't his business and he knew it must be a painful topic for her to dwell upon. In that moment she looked so sad and vulnerable. So very alone. And a fierce emotion rose upward inside him. The desire to protect and keep her safe forevermore.

At first, he thought she wouldn't respond. Then she spoke in an aching whisper as she confirmed what he'd been told.

"*Ja*, it is true. I cannot have children," she said.

His heart gave a powerful squeeze. How he wished he could take away her pain. He wished he hadn't dredged it all up again. Yet, he felt compelled to ask.

"I know it must upset you terribly, but the Lord has a way of providing for all our needs. You must not give up hope," he said.

She snorted. "I don't see how the Lord can provide me with kids."

"I don't, either, but I do know *Gott* has never let me down. I thought He had, but I was wrong. I hope you'll give Him a chance to work wonders in your life," he said.

She frowned and glanced at him but didn't respond. They were friends and had a sort of bond between them, but he'd pushed her too far today. Way too far.

"I'm sorry for frightening you. The last thing I wanted to do was cause you any distress," he said.

"*Danke,*" she said, her voice sounding small.

"Caroline, I… I'd like us to be more than friends," he said.

"What do you mean?" she asked.

"I… I have romantic feelings for you," he said.

"*Ne!* Don't say that."

"I mean it, Caroline. I have deep feelings for you and I'd like to court you with the intention of marriage."

There. He'd finally said what was in his heart. Now it was in her hands.

"That isn't possible. I don't want to marry you. Not ever," she said with such finality.

"I know you're afraid, but I think we could…"

She shook her head. "I said *ne*."

"May I ask why?"

"I… I don't want to be married without knowing I can have *kinder*. Maybe you can, but I can't," she said.

"But don't you think we could—"

She cut him off. "Please, let's drop it. Nothing is going to change, and I don't want to keep hashing it over."

Okay, he got it. Even though he'd made it clear her inability to have children didn't matter to him, it obviously still mattered to her and he had no idea how to convince her otherwise. He wished she could be happy with just him, but he couldn't blame her for wanting more.

They didn't speak the rest of the ride home. And when he helped her out of the buggy and watched her go inside her uncle's farmhouse, he breathed a sigh of relief. At least she was safe. For now. But what about tomorrow or next week? She'd have to drive back and forth to school every day and go into town on errands. How could he protect her from people like Rand Henbury? How could he ever ensure that she and the other people he loved were okay?

He couldn't! And though he'd been taught that whatever happened was *Gott's* will, he struggled to accept that. Because they each had freedom of choice. Even people like Rand could choose to do works of goodness or works of darkness. But it was Ben's job to have enough faith to accept whatever came his way. And that was easier said than done. But he now knew that, no matter what anger he might face in the future, he didn't need to fight back. He also knew that he longed for Caroline with all his heart, but she didn't feel the same. Now he prayed for the strength to accept that.

But he feared it might be the most difficult thing he'd ever had to do.

Chapter Twelve

Caroline shivered as she pulled her gray scarf tighter around her throat. Sitting in the buggy, she gripped the leather lead lines, her gloves doing very little to warm her frozen fingers. The early-morning air felt frigid, the sun barely peeking over the eastern hills. Ice crystals clung to spindly tree limbs lining the county road. The fields and mountains surrounding the valley were covered in pristine white for miles around. It had snowed in the night. Just two inches, but it was enough to make the roads slick with a sheet of ice, though not enough for her to cancel school.

It had been two days since she'd seen Ben and she missed him, she couldn't deny it. But it was for the best. Wasn't it?

She focused on the snowplow markers at the side of the road, keeping the horse even with the shoulder so he didn't pull them into the ditch. Though it had been dark and cold, she'd left the house early on purpose, before Ben had arrived to drive her to school. After his declaration of intent to court her, she'd decided it was time she became more independent. Time she drove the buggy and got herself around without help. But this was the first time she'd driven since her injury. On the one hand, it felt good to be by herself. The tug of the horse gave her a feeling of exhilaration and freedom. But on the other, it reminded her of how vulnerable she was and that bad things could happen when she least expected them.

Shaking off that morbid thought, she took a deep inhale and held it a moment before letting it go. She could see a puff of her breath on the chilly air. Her heavy woolen cloak was more than welcome today. She'd also folded a heavy quilt around her legs but still felt the cold emanating into the cab of the buggy.

She wondered what Ben and Bishop Yoder might say once they found out she'd driven herself today. And then, in spite of her desire not to, she marveled at how much she missed Ben's presence. She'd grown used to him always being by her side. He never talked much, but she realized with some surprise how comfortable she felt when she was around him. He made her feel safe and calm, which was just another reason for them to separate. She couldn't marry him. There was no use discussing it. And now that she could walk well on her own, it was time to let him go.

As she pulled into the schoolyard, the horse and wheels of the buggy dug deep trails in the unspoiled snow. She drove to the back before climbing out and stabling the animal in the small horse shed. Taking deep breaths, she slogged through the snow to the schoolhouse, grateful that she'd worn her black snow boots. She quickly swept off the front steps, then went inside and started a nice fire in the potbellied stove. She'd get the classroom toasty warm and everything ready for the children before she went outside to shovel the walk paths.

She'd just finished writing the day's lesson assignments on the blackboard when she heard the scrape of a shovel outside. Peering out the window, she saw Ben clearing the driveway. He was dressed in a heavy coat, the edge of a knit cap peeking out from beneath the rim of his black felt hat. Like her, he wore gloves and boots as he pushed the snow shovel easily to remove the layer of white from the stone walk paths.

Hmm. Even though she'd left without him this morning, he'd followed her here. She'd hoped he'd take the hint and leave her alone.

Still wearing her warm cloak, she stepped outside and wrapped her arms around herself. It was more a protective gesture than one of warmth. She wasn't sure what to say to him.

He paused in his work and leaned against the handle of the snow shovel. Looking up at her, he smiled, but it didn't quite reach his eyes. Without him saying one word, she knew he wasn't happy that she'd left without him that morning or that she'd rebuffed his offer of marriage.

"*Guder mariye,*" she called, unable to infuse her voice with much cheer. After all, she didn't want to encourage him.

"*Hallo*, Caroline. You left without me this morning," he said.

She almost laughed, wondering how he always seemed to know exactly what she was thinking. His candor didn't surprise her at all. If she'd learned nothing else about this man during the weeks they'd been working together, it was that he was blunt and forthright and usually said what was on his mind.

"I really appreciate all that you've done for me, Ben," she said. "But I don't need your help anymore. I'm walking just fine on my own and can do these chores by myself. You should concentrate on your own work now."

There. That was good, wasn't it?

A flash of hurt filled his eyes and he looked away, gazing at the thin creek bed where crystals of ice coated every available surface. Maybe she'd been too direct and hurt his feelings, which wasn't what she wanted. Not after all he'd done for her.

"I'm afraid I can't do that, Caroline. The bishop hasn't released me from my assignment yet. And it'll make things much easier on you if I shovel the walkways. It'll give your legs time to really heal," he said, his voice soft and undemanding, yet holding a note of authority.

Everything he said was true. Although she was getting along nicely, all it would take was a little fall to undo weeks of improvement. And she realized she sounded ungrateful. After all, he'd made window boxes for her and put up all the new playground equipment and helped her with Seth and Mary. He'd definitely gone above and beyond the call of duty, and she appreciated it. She truly did. But they'd become too close. They'd confided things to each other that they'd told nobody else. And she'd come to realize that was dangerous to her heart. Because in spite of her will to remain aloof, she'd fallen for this man.

She hadn't realized it all at once, like a bolt of lightning. The knowledge had snuck up on her like a thief in the night. It had occurred to her last evening as she'd said her prayers and climbed into bed that she looked forward to seeing him today. And that was when she knew. She cared deeply for this big, gruff man, in spite of all that he'd done. But even if he truly had become a peace-loving pacifist, they could have no future together. Because she could never give him a child.

And even though he said that didn't matter, she knew in her heart that it did. Because she still wanted children. She wanted to be a mother and she wanted Ben to be a father. Becoming parents was ingrained in both of them since the day they were born. They had been raised to know they would someday be parents. And now that wasn't possible, she had no idea how to get past it or stop longing for it in her life. And even though Ben said he was okay with it, she feared he would come to resent her for it. Maybe not at first, but later in the future. He'd see other men's children and know what he was missing and she couldn't stand the thought that he might come to resent her. He deserved to find and marry another woman who could give him kids.

"You're right, of course," she said. "*Danke* for all your help. I appreciate you shoveling the snow. But once you're finished, you should go *heemet* and help the bishop with your chores there. I have no need for you to stay around here anymore."

A frown tugged at his forehead. "I will go after I've chopped some firewood, but I'll be back later this afternoon to ensure you get home safely."

She heaved a little huff of exasperation. He was

being stubborn. Before she could argue the point, the rattle of another buggy coming into the yard drew their attention. In unison, they looked up.

Darrin Albrecht, the deacon of their congregation, waved as he pulled up in front of the schoolhouse. Six of his school-age children poured out of the buggy wearing a variety of boots, hats, scarves and gloves. The air was suddenly filled with laughter and the voices of children as they hurried inside the warm building. And Caroline was grateful for the distraction.

She focused her energy on the kids, ushering them inside and helping them doff their heavy winter clothing. She ignored Ben, forcing herself not to look back at him as she closed the door. She didn't want to talk to him anymore. Didn't want to feel close to him or depend on him or confide any more of her concerns and fears in him. It was time to pull back.

Because she cared for him, she must let him go. Because he deserved to marry a woman who could make him a father. And whether Ben and Bishop Yoder agreed with her or not, it was time for her to be on her own.

Ben watched as Caroline disappeared inside with the children. She didn't look back at him, though he couldn't help wishing she would. As he resumed his shoveling, it wasn't long before more children arrived. They all waved at him and he stopped to chat with each of their fathers. Funny how he'd become much better friends with all of them since Caroline had entered his life. Maybe it was because they saw him every day here at the school and were getting used to him. No doubt their children told them about his work here, too. Maybe they were finally starting to accept him.

Ben's uncle Amos and Mervin Schwartz pulled into the yard at the same time, followed by the Geingerich *familye*.

"*Guder mariye*, Ben," Mervin called.

Ben lifted a hand in greeting.

Normally, the older children drove their younger siblings or their mothers brought them to school. But today they all knew about Rand Henbury's escapades. Ben had reported everything to his uncle, and word had soon spread. With the slick condition of the roads, the fathers wanted to protect their children.

The kids hopped out of the conveyances and greeted each other with eager waves. From his position near the woodpile, Ben watched Seth and Mary with eagle eyes. Mary wasn't much of an issue. She was sweet, young and trusting, and the little girl was all smiles as she glommed onto Rachel Geingerich. Their squealing laughter rang through the air as they raced to the front door.

"Hi, Ben!" Seth waved at him.

"*Hallo!*" Ben returned. His heart lightened considerably when Seth joined Sam King and Andrew Yoder. Though the two other boys were a year older, Seth towered over them. They didn't seem to mind as he smiled and went inside with them.

Whew! Just that small greeting meant everything to Ben. It was such a vast improvement over Seth's previous actions that Ben realized they'd made great headway in helping the boy overcome his anger and resentment at the world.

Ben was surprised when his uncle Amos got out of his buggy and walked over to him.

"I'm glad you're here to look after things at the school," the bishop said.

Ben gazed at the path he'd created in the snow, noticing that the moisture was already starting to melt.

"Caroline doesn't want me here. She drove herself today," Ben said.

The bishop's mouth tightened as he considered this. "*Ach*, it doesn't matter. As long as you're here and she and the *kinder* are safe, that's what's most important. Because of that *Englisch* boy, the roads aren't safe anymore. Though I don't want to do it, I may need to pay a visit to the sheriff in town. Maybe he can speak to the young man and his *vadder*."

Ben nodded, surprised that his uncle had confided in him. It was another sign of trust. The bishop had heard about the confrontation between Ben and Rand and knew that Ben had not fought back. And with a zap of delight, Ben couldn't help feeling for the first time like he truly belonged here.

"*Ach*, we'll be back to pick up the kids from school. You take care," Bishop Yoder said.

With a nod, he turned and walked away. Likewise, the other fathers pulled out of the yard to return home. Ben watched them go, feeling happy and sad at the same time. Happy because he really thought he could spend the rest of his life here in this *Gmay*. These were his people. But a feeling of despair overshadowed his joy because he had no one to share his life with. No home and *familye* of his own.

Caroline didn't want him.

If only she could accept him, they might have a chance at happiness together. No, she couldn't give him children, but marriage was more than that, wasn't it? Still, her actions that morning had spoken volumes. Even after all the time they'd spent together, she wanted nothing to do with him. When they'd been confronted with Rand Henbury in town the other day, she thought Ben was still prone to violence. That he was ready to fight. And knowing that he'd once killed a man, she wanted nothing to do with him. She wished he'd go away and leave her alone.

He had thought, with time, that Caroline would come to know and understand what was truly inside his heart. But now he could see that she didn't really need his help here at the school. At least, not all day long. He could go home and help his uncle with the many chores waiting for him there. He could even make plans and start to develop his own farmland. But he didn't know what he'd use it for. Why bother when he had no one to share it with and nothing to look forward to? He had friends in this *Gmay* now and knew he could marry one of their other young women. He owned land and could build a home and provide for a family. But he didn't want another woman. He wanted Caroline. No one else could ever satisfy his heart.

Lifting the ax, he took his frustration out on the woodpile by chopping enough kindling to last several days. Finally, he put the ax away in the shed so it wouldn't rust and made his way over to his horse and buggy. He'd leave and return later that afternoon, when it was time for Caroline to go home. Whether she wanted him here or not, he felt bound by the bishop's word and must ensure she arrived home safely that evening. He couldn't stand the thought that Rand Henbury might harm her and was determined to be here for her.

As he passed by the pretty window boxes he'd built for Caroline, he saw her inside. She stood in front of the chalkboard, holding an open book in her hands. She was speaking to the class, though he couldn't hear her words. She must have caught his movement because she turned her head and glanced at him. For several moments her eyes locked with his. Then she turned her back on him and walked to the other side of the classroom, where he couldn't see her anymore. She'd dismissed him like she would a recalcitrant scholar.

His heart gave a painful squeeze. After all these years, he'd begun to think he would never find someone he cared about enough to settle down with. But he'd been wrong. And he realized Caroline was special the moment he set eyes on her, long before the accident that nearly took her life. And because she was so special to him, he must let her go.

As soon as he got home, he'd talk to his uncle Amos about rescinding his assignment to accompany Caroline and tend to the needs of the school. Ben hated the thought of not seeing Caroline every day, but he also realized that seeing her all the time was making the pain even worse. It was like holding out a sumptuous banquet to a starving man and telling him he couldn't eat one single morsel.

Yes, it was time for Ben to go. He must leave her alone and let her live her own life, even if it was the hardest thing he'd ever faced.

Chapter Thirteen

That afternoon Caroline expected to harness her horse and buggy before driving herself home. But when she stepped outside after all the kids had left for the day, Ben had her buggy waiting and ready to go.

She shouldn't be surprised. If nothing else, she'd learned that Ben was quiet but strong-willed. He never forced his will on her, *per se*. She usually voiced her objection, he quietly listened and then he did whatever he wanted anyway.

Stepping out onto the top landing of the stairs, she glanced at him before making a pretense of tugging on her gloves and locking the front door. His own horse and buggy stood just behind hers, and she had no doubt he was going to follow her—all the way home.

The thought made her smile, and she realized how well she knew this man. But then she remembered her resolve to send him away and forced her lips into a stern frown.

"You don't need to wait for me anymore, Ben. I don't need you here. Please, go away," she said.

She ignored the flash of pain that filled his eyes and picked up her bookbag. She hated to hurt him but knew it was for the best. He must leave her alone. She was already mourning the thought of losing him and didn't want to make things worse.

Concentrating on her feet, she walked down the steps with little trouble. Though she could negotiate the stairs with ease, it was a habit to watch what she was doing. It felt so good to move freely. To feel steady and strong. Her heart delighted in how easy it was to walk without a cane, and she promised herself she would never take her legs and the ability to walk for granted again. *Gott* had been so good to her and yet, she wanted more. Much, much more. A loving husband and *familye* of her own. Children and a man to shower her love upon. But it was never to be, so she should accept it and move on. She must have faith that *Gott* had something else in store for her with the schoolchildren. It would be enough. It must be!

Ben didn't say a word as he opened the door and held out his arm to assist her in case she needed it. But she didn't touch him. Without another word, she moved past him and climbed inside before pulling the door closed with a final snap of the latch. Out of her peripheral vision, she saw Ben step back, looking a bit surprised. She ignored him, forcing herself to look straight ahead. Taking the lead lines in a practiced grip, she released the brake.

Just as school had let out for the day, it had started to snow again. Gigantic flakes of white floated through the air, turning the fields into a lovely, brisk winter wonderland. She figured she had just enough time to get home safely before it started coming down in earnest.

Without giving Ben time to get into his own buggy, she slapped the lines against the horse's back, and the buggy lurched forward. In her rearview mirror, she saw Ben scurrying to climb inside his own buggy and come after her. And she would have laughed out loud if it didn't make her so sad. In her heart of hearts, she wished he were sitting right beside her, listening as she chatted about the weather, the upcoming school Christmas program and how Mary and Seth were making so much great progress. Ben would undoubtedly give her that sidelong, mischievous look of his whenever she said something contrary or impertinent. How she wished she dared take his arm and hold on tight forever. But that couldn't be reality. Not for a woman like her.

As she pulled out of the schoolyard, she saw Ben's buggy following right behind. In spite of the questionable road conditions, he urged his horse into a fast trot to keep up. Knowing he was nearby provided her a bit of comfort, but her heart felt extra heavy today. She knew the bishop was planning to come over to her uncle's home later that evening to discuss using Mervin's little sawmill to cut timber for a new shed on his property. She was determined to confront both men and insist that she no longer needed a bodyguard. Somehow, she had to make them both understand. And yet, she did need Ben, if only to continue being her best friend in the whole wide world.

No! She mustn't think that way. It was time to plead her case and have Bishop Yoder rescind Ben's assignment to look after her and the school. Because, if she really acknowledged the truth, it was starting to break her heart. Having him near all the time and knowing they could never be more than friends was almost more than she could stand. It wasn't fair to Ben, either. After all, he had his own life to look forward to. His land needed clearing if he was going to start up his own farm. He'd need to build a house and barn and plant crops in the spring, which meant he might accompany the bishop to her home tonight to talk about using Uncle Mervin's sawmill for his own needs.

The thought of seeing him again made her heart give a powerful leap. But she mustn't give in to the excitement. Nothing could ever come of it. There were a couple of pretty girls in their *Gmay* that Ben could ask out. At church this past Sunday, she had seen them eyeing him with interest. It seemed that, with the arrival of Mary and Seth, they'd heard about Ben's kindness to the kids and no longer feared him. He should marry one of them. But the thought of Ben paying court to someone else made Caroline jealous. She could hardly stand to think that she wouldn't be a part of his life anymore, but it was for the best. Because she loved him, she wanted him to be happy. She had to let him go.

The blaring of a horn startled her out of her thoughts. She jerked her head up and stared into the rearview mirror. Ben was right behind her. But as the road made a slight incline, she saw the outline of Rand Henbury's black pickup truck following too closely behind Ben's horse and buggy.

Oh, no! Not again! The guy was relentless.

That old feeling of absolute terror rose in her throat with the speed of a fist to the gut. Her hands trembled and she took a deep breath, trying to settle her nerves. But then something hardened inside her. What right did Rand Henbury, or any man, have to make her fearful? None whatsoever. Not if she didn't give them that power over her.

Caroline dug deep inside herself, determined not to be afraid anymore. The roads were damp and slick. The snow was no longer melting, but rather, sticking to the asphalt. With the shorter days of winter, the sun was quickly fading. Nightfall was coming on and the sky looked dark and foreboding. In the short time since she'd left the schoolhouse, the temperature had dropped and the roads were freezing with black ice. The horn blasted again and she fought to control her skittish horse.

Why wouldn't Rand just leave them alone? While he seemed to like hassling anyone he could, she feared she and Ben had become his main targets. No doubt Rand had noticed when and where they'd be traveling along the county roads each day, and he seemed to take particular delight in spooking her horse.

Looking up, Caroline saw that she was fast approaching the one-lane bridge that crossed over the Arkansas River. With the rainstorm they'd had over the past couple of days, the river was swollen and choppy. There was room enough on the narrow bridge for only one vehicle to cross at a time. The guardrails were rather thin, and it wasn't a place she wanted to be caught with Rand's speeding truck.

Deciding she'd rather be stuck all night in a snowdrift
than risk being killed in another accident, she gripped
the lead lines tighter and slowed her horse. Clicking
her tongue, she pulled the animal over on the shoulder as far as she dared and hoped Rand would pass her
by. She noticed Ben did the same, following her every
movement as he pulled up close behind her. It seemed
a protective gesture on his part, as if he were defend-
ing her. And though she was nervous and jittery right
now, it gave her comfort to know he was there with her.

Rand didn't slow down. Not one bit. In fact, he
speeded up, blasting his horn again as he veered into
the other lane to pass them. As he zipped by, he rolled
his window down about six inches and yelled obsceni-
ties at her. Caroline's ears burned with repulsion, and
she realized he wasn't paying attention to his driving.
Staring after him, she thought he must be insane. What
was wrong with him? Driving like a lunatic on these
dangerous roads. What had happened in his life to make
him so careless?

Rand almost made the bridge, but his truck skidded
on the black ice at the last moment. He lost control as
his vehicle slid sideways and sideswiped the guardrail,
sending his truck crashing into the icy river.

Caroline gasped and stared in horror as the truck
quickly tipped upward and began to sink. It took only
moments for it to go under, the water spinning around
the truck like a whirlpool. The last thing Caroline saw
before the vehicle was completely submerged was
Rand's pale face frozen in shock and terror. And the
awful truth of his predicament dawned on her. Rand

couldn't crawl out the open window. It wasn't wide enough for him to fit through. Unless he could get the door open or kick out the glass, he was trapped inside his truck. He would drown!

She had to do something to help him. And fast!

She reached to get out of the buggy, but the door was suddenly yanked open and Ben stuck his head inside. She blinked in surprise and wonder. She'd never seen him looking so urgent before.

"Are you *allrecht*?" he asked, his eyes wide and anxious as they scanned her for injury.

"*Ja*, I'm okay but…" She didn't get to finish.

"*Gut!* Stay here where you'll be safe and warm." He slammed the door closed and raced toward the river.

She watched as he stood beside the embankment, as if considering his options. With swift movements, he shed his coat, hat and boots, tossing them carelessly aside in the snow. Then he dived headfirst into the icy water. The river closed over him, seeming to swallow him whole. A slight splash rose upward in the air in his wake.

"*Ne*, Ben!" she yelled, but too late.

He was gone. She hurried out of the buggy and raced over to the bridge, not caring in the least that he'd told her to stay put or that it was now snowing hard. Snowflakes landed on her cheeks and eyelashes but she didn't even feel the chill. Already, Ben had been under too long. He couldn't last. Not in this cold.

"Ben! Ben!" she screamed over and over again, scanning the surface of the water for some sign of him. But she saw nothing except choppy water.

Her thoughts scattered, though one pounded her

mind. She'd lost him for good. The frigid temperatures would steal his strength. He wouldn't be able to survive. He would drown while trying to save Rand's life.

And that was when she knew the truth. Ben wasn't a violent man. He'd been young and frightened and pushed beyond his ability to cope. He'd fought back, not because he was vicious or mean but simply because he'd been scared and wanted to defend his dear mother.

She'd been working with him for weeks now. She'd witnessed his gentle ways and kind deeds over and over again. If he'd been a lesser man, he would have walked away from their faith and gone to live in the *Englisch* world. He could have escaped so much ridicule and hardship simply by leaving. But he'd stayed and faced it all with a quiet contrition that had impressed her beyond measure. She'd seen the truth in his eyes when he'd told her of his regrets. He was filled with the love of *Gott*, not the violence she so abhorred. Surely, he wouldn't have jumped in to save a bully like Rand if he wasn't good inside.

But even if she could give him children and they could be together always, the revelation had come too late. Because now he would die, and she'd never get to see him again.

She was vaguely aware of a car pulling off to the side of the road. An *Englisch* woman got out and ran over to her.

"What's happened?" the woman asked.

A man driving a truck joined them on the bridge. Caroline explained but had no idea what she said to them. She only knew one thing. She'd lost Ben. Lost him for good. And she was sick with the knowledge that she'd never get to say goodbye. Never get to tell him how much she truly loved him.

Yes, she loved him! She knew that now with absolute clarity. But it was too late because she'd never get to tell him how much.

The *Englisch* woman pulled out her cell phone and dialed for help while the man went to the water's edge to see what he could do. But Caroline didn't move. She stayed right where she was, her gaze scanning the murky water below for any sign of Ben. Nothing. Just a revolving vortex of freezing water.

And in her heart, she knew she had not only lost Ben Yoder that day. She had also lost the love of her life.

Ben grit his teeth the moment the freezing water enfolded him in its icy grip. Needles of pain dotted his flesh as he moved his arms and kicked his legs. He fought on, struggling to swim against the heavy current. Fighting for all he was worth. Because he had to save Rand. In that moment it didn't matter that the man was a bully. Nor did it matter that he was an *Englischer*. Rand was still one of *Gott's* children and Ben couldn't let him die. Not without trying to save him. Not this time.

Ben stared into the darkness, trying to see the truck as the water carried it down, down to the bottom of the river. The water rushed past Ben, trying to pull him with it. At first, he fought the undertow. But then he realized it could save his energy—or spell his doom.

He let it sweep him along. Then he swam fast and hard, trying to reach Rand. He grit his teeth and held his breath, until he thought his lungs would burst. The cold was sapping his energy. He was weakening! He had only moments before he'd be forced to give up the fight and rise to the surface. In the blackness, he lost sight of the truck. Where was it? Where was Rand?

There! A silvery shadow gleamed against the vehicle. It had thumped to the bottom of the river, sending up a cloud of mud that he couldn't see through. As he swam lower, the current didn't seem as strong and he was able to touch the front fender of the truck. Grabbing on to the grill and then the side mirror, Ben pulled himself over to the door of the driver's seat. He calmed himself, watching for another glimmer of light. Rand was inside the truck but looked unconscious. The cab had filled with water, which Ben thought was a blessing. It would equalize the pressure inside the cab and allow him to open the door.

He tugged on the handle but the door wouldn't open. Gripping the handle, he braced his bare feet against the side of the vehicle and pulled with all his might, vaguely aware that the current had pulled his socks off his feet.

Finally, the door gave and opened sluggishly, as if in slow motion. Letting it go, Ben clawed at Rand to pull him free of the vehicle. Although the Amish didn't own or drive any vehicles, they still rode in them occasionally when they had to travel great distances. Ben knew the layout and was grateful Rand wasn't wearing a seat belt that he would need to struggle to release.

As he pulled Rand out into the flow of the river and thrashed to get him to the surface, Ben's lungs burned for oxygen. His muscles cramped with cold and fatigue. He was weakening and feared he couldn't make it. Feared he'd never see his sweet Caroline again. Never hear her tinkling laughter or share another gentle kiss.

He kicked his legs, refusing to stop. Refusing to give in without a fight. He broke the surface and inhaled a deep breath. Waves of choppy water slapped him in the face and clogged his throat. He coughed, fighting to pull Rand to the shore. And suddenly, there were other hands there to take over for him. Men and women he didn't know took the weight of Rand's body from him—strangers who understood the situation was a matter of life and death.

Ben lay there gasping and coughing for breath, too exhausted to move, ignoring the pain as rocks dug into his skin. He was vaguely aware of a man rolling Rand onto his back before performing CPR. Rand looked pale as death, and Ben feared he'd been too late to save him. Too slow and weak to get him to the surface in time.

Rand jerked suddenly and gave a low gurgle as water ran from his mouth. Then he began to hack and spew water. He was alive! He wasn't dead at all. And then he was crying and coughing some more.

A cheer rang out among the small crowd of people. Ben lifted his head, wondering where they had all come from. They must have been driving along the road and saw the accident and stopped to help. But where was Caroline? Was she all right?

He tried to stand but slumped against the pebbled shore, lying among the rocks, snow and ice, too weak to move. He lost track of time, feeling as if he were living a nightmare. Someone laid a blanket over him but he couldn't get warm. He was shivering until he thought his teeth might rattle and break. He vaguely heard the shrill whine of a siren and knew the police and an ambulance had arrived. A paramedic and EMT started working on Rand.

Ben jerked in surprise when Eli Stoltzfus leaned over him. His foggy brain reminded him that Eli was an Amish paramedic who worked with the small hospital in town to help their people. It was so good to see a friendly face, but he couldn't tell Eli that. He mouthed the words but his voice was only a low croak.

"Ben, can you hear me?" Eli asked in English.

Ben nodded.

"*Gut!* We're gonna get you warm and take you for a ride in the ambulance. You stay with me, okay? Don't go to sleep. Don't you leave me," Eli repeated over and over again.

"Car... Caroline." Ben finally got her name out and struggled to sit up. He fell back. He couldn't understand what was wrong with him.

"She's fine, Ben. Just lie back and let me help you," Eli said.

And that was when Ben saw her. Looking up, he gazed at the darkened sky above, wondering if he would meet his Savior this very night. At first, he couldn't see anything except a swirl of snowflakes as they fell upon his face. He was aware of the moisture but he wasn't cold anymore. In fact, he couldn't feel anything now. Not his arms or legs. Not even his heart.

Caroline stood alone on the bridge above. From this distance, her face appeared gaunt and pale. He could just make out her features; she looked worried and near tears. How he hated to see her cry. He longed to stand and go to her, to hold and comfort her and get her to smile. To convince her that they should be together. He tried to lift his hand to beckon to her but his body felt too numb. His limbs wouldn't obey his will. He couldn't move at all.

And that was when Ben realized he was in danger, too. He wasn't shivering anymore. In fact, he felt pleasantly warm and lethargic. As if he were apart from his body, floating on air. No doubt hypothermia had set in. Even though he was out of the water, he still might die. But nothing mattered more than Caroline being okay. She meant so much to him. She meant everything. If only he could make her understand what was in his heart and mind. How much he loved and adored her. But she wanted a better man than him. She'd made that very clear over and over. It was what she deserved. And more than anything, he wished he could go back in time and change what he had done. Because his actions had pilfered his future happiness. They had stolen every chance he had of a joyous life with Caroline.

The shadows crowded closer, but he tried to fight them off. He wandered in and out of consciousness. Eli's insistent voice called him back each time he tried to sleep. And the only thought that kept him going was the knowledge that Caroline was safe.

He tried to lift his head, to see her on the bridge again. But she wasn't there. Good. She was out of the wet and cold. Oh, how he longed to see her again. To hear her voice and laughter. To see her face as she concentrated on a particularly difficult math problem on the chalkboard. He could die happy if only he could feast his eyes upon her sweet face one last time.

But he knew even that would never satisfy him. No other woman had ever made him feel the way she did. Like he could do anything he set his mind to. He wanted none other. Even getting warm didn't matter now. Not when he couldn't have her.

Chapter Fourteen

"You're not coming inside to see Ben with us?"

Caroline shook her head. Little Mary's question took her off guard. She didn't want to meet the child's steady gaze. It was too bold. Too inquiring.

A variety of fears and failings whooshed around in Caroline's mind. She didn't want to face them. Not now, not ever. And yet, her faith taught her to trust in *Gott* and have a calm heart. But that was not how she felt. Not for a long time now.

They stood outside the small cinder-block hospital in town. It was early afternoon, the day after Ben had jumped into the river to save Rand Henbury. It had snowed in the night, laying down another two inches of white stuff. If not for that, they would have been here earlier. But now the sky was crystal clear, not a cloud in sight. The sun blazed from the sky, melting off the roads and sidewalks—a lull before a more serious storm was scheduled to hit their area in a couple more days.

Eli Stoltzfus, their Amish paramedic, had come to their farm earlier that morning to give them a report.

Thankfully, Ben would be all right, but Caroline found she still couldn't stop worrying about him, much as she wished to. They'd also had a wonderful visit from Sharon Wedge, the *Englisch* woman from Child Protective Services. She'd informed them that Mary and Seth were theirs and could stay with them for good. As if they'd expected anything less.

"We have too many people to visit Ben all at once. You go on in and see him. I'll wait for you here," Caroline said.

Truth be known, Caroline was dying to see Ben. But knowing he was safe and would recover from his ordeal would have to be enough for now. Talking to him after all they'd been through would feel awkward now. And honestly, she feared she might relent and ask him to stay with her forever. What good would that do either of them? It would only lead to more misery and pain.

Aunt Hannah and Uncle Mervin stood on the front steps nearby. From their expressions, she knew they were concerned. For Ben and for her. But what did they expect? That she would fall into Ben's arms and they'd live happily ever after? Life didn't happen that way. Not for her.

"*Komm* on, Mary. Let's go in." Hannah beckoned to the child. Mary scowled but obediently took the woman's hand.

Caroline stared after the girl, her mind churning. When Mary and Seth had heard that Ben was in danger, they'd been inconsolable. Uncle Mervin had finally agreed to let them see the man and know for sure that he would be all right. Because the two orphans had already been through so much, no one wanted to add any more drama or uncertainty to their lives.

Forcing a smile on her face, Caroline walked over to her aunt and reached out to take baby Susan. Cradling the little girl close, Caroline smiled at Mary and Seth. "Besides, someone has to stay with Susan. A *boppli* can't go into the hospital because they're too young. There are too many germs for her to catch."

There. That was a good argument, wasn't it? Caroline was certain her logic was correct, even if they could have left Susan home with her fourteen-year-old sister.

At that moment Bishop Yoder walked outside the hospital. He was accompanied by an older *Englisch* man whose mouth was curled in a look of contrition. His legs were slightly bowlegged from riding a horse, and his face looked weathered by age and hard work. He wore a dusty, beat-up cowboy hat, blue jeans, a long Western coat and scuffed boots, along with a rather severe expression on his face. When he saw them, he paused. Then he brushed past them with a single nod of respect.

"*Hallo*, Bishop!" Mervin greeted the man.

"*Hallo.* Are you going in to see Ben?" the bishop asked.

"*Ja.* Wasn't that Garth Henbury with you?" Uncle Mervin asked.

Bishop Yoder nodded, his gaze following the man as he walked down the street.

"You mean that's Rand Henbury's father?" Hannah asked.

Both the bishop and Mervin nodded.

"I've just had a long chat with him. He knows Rand has been terrifying the Amish and that Ben saved his life last night. He's grateful and has promised that Rand will never cause any more trouble to our people from now on."

Caroline sighed with relief. "That's nice to know. I hope he means it."

Bishop Yoder nodded. "I do, too. But Rand will have to decide that for himself. I hope he's grateful and realizes he has a second chance to make things right in his life."

Caroline hoped so, too. Nothing else needed to be said. They all knew Garth was the richest rancher in the area, but he sure didn't look the part. He was a stern, hardworking man who could buy almost anything he wanted. He had a reputation for demanding perfection from his workers, but when it came to his son, he made lots of exceptions. But this time, Rand's foolishness had almost gotten him killed.

"Rand is an only child," the bishop said. "Apparently, his *mudder* died when he was very young."

They each nodded, having heard this before. Whenever Rand got into trouble, which was quite often these days, Garth and his high-priced attorney from Denver got him off. It seemed that Garth refused to believe his son could do any wrong. Even if the Amish were prone to suing other people, Garth wasn't a man they wanted to tangle with. But this time was different. Apparently, Garth planned to rethink his actions on behalf of his son and do something about it. At least, that was what Caroline hoped would happen.

"I drew a picture of our farm for Ben." Mary broke into Caroline's thoughts as she held up a piece of paper.

With the innocence of her youth, the girl had no idea

why she should be concerned by Garth Henbury's presence and barely paid the man any heed.

Mary's picture had been drawn with crayons and showed the rudimentary scribbles of a two-story red log house, barn and farmyard. Because the Amish did not believe in making graven images of themselves, no people were shown in the drawing. Just trees, flowers and farm animals.

Seth snorted. "Why did you draw flowers? It snowed and buried all of them yesterday. We don't got no flowers in our yard now."

"We don't have *any* flowers in our yard now." Caroline corrected his poor grammar. Then she leaned over to get a better look at the picture. "*Ach*, that's a lovely drawing. I'm sure Ben will like it just as it is. It'll remind him of spring."

"Come on, Mary. Let's go. I want to see Ben," Seth grumbled. He had joined Aunt Hannah on the steps, looking anxious to go inside.

"I'm coming." Smiling with satisfaction, the girl skipped up the steps, her picture waving in the breeze. The wide double doors swooshed open, and just before she went inside, Mary turned and waved goodbye.

Caroline smiled and waved back, then pulled her warm woolen cloak tighter at her throat. Oh, how she loved these two sweet children. How she loved life. *Gott* had been good to her and Ben yesterday. He'd kept them safe.

Her *familye* disappeared inside, leaving her alone with the bishop.

"You're not going in to see Ben?" the man asked.

She took a deep breath, trying to gather her courage

as she met the bishop's unwavering eyes. "*Ne*. I think it's best if I wait here with the *boppli*."

Bishop Yoder's gaze held hers for several moments. "I see."

"How is he?" she couldn't help asking.

"*Gut*. He'll be able to *komm* home tomorrow. They treated him for hypothermia and frostbite, but he'll be all right," the bishop said.

Frostbite!

"Are you sure he's okay?" she asked.

"*Ja*, he wouldn't let the doctors amputate until they were absolutely certain they couldn't save all his fingers and toes. Eli supported him in that quest. And now it looks like they were wise. The circulation has returned and it appears all is well."

Caroline released a long exhale, only just realizing she'd been holding her breath. She hated the thought of Ben losing any of his digits. With a lifetime of farm chores ahead of him, he'd need strong hands and feet to do his work.

"I'm so glad," she said, meaning every word.

"Apparently, it was touch and go for Rand Henbury. Everyone feared he might die. But he is conscious now and was even able to speak to his *vadder* for a while. He's sorry for what he did. I have also offered Mr. Henbury our help in any way we can."

"Hmm. He didn't look too pleased to see us Amish here," she said.

A slight smile curved the bishop's lips. "He wasn't pleased. Especially not when he found out his son has been harassing the Amish people nonstop. Apparently, some of the townsfolk had complained to the police, and the sheriff spoke to Mr. Henbury. He refused to listen. But after what happened last night, I saw a different side to him today that wasn't there before."

She shifted the baby on her hip and tilted her head. "Oh?"

"*Ja*, this time he was afraid he might lose his son. I can't be sure, but I think Mr. Henbury will do as he said and put an end to the abuse. If Rand persists in his actions, we might not have as happy an ending the next time around."

"*Ja*, that's true," she said, relieved that both Rand and Ben would be okay.

"Although Rand is coherent and doesn't seem to have suffered any brain damage from his ordeal, he now has pneumonia. The doctor has put him on oxygen and it appears he will be in the hospital for a while longer," Bishop Yoder said.

"That's what Eli told us this morning," she said.

The bishop lifted his bushy eyebrows in question. "Eli paid you a visit?"

She nodded. "I'm sorry to hear that Rand isn't out of danger yet."

"The doctors are giving him the best care. You really should go inside and visit Ben."

His words shocked her. He was a kind, good man and their unconditional leader. She hated to defy him in anything.

"*Ach*, I can't, Bishop Yoder. Please don't ask it of me. And you should tell Ben that he doesn't need to look after me and the school. Truly, I can get along fine on my own. I don't need him anymore," she said.

Her words hung in the air like a gigantic, frosty

cloud. It was true she didn't need Ben. But she supposed she didn't need anyone. Not to live and breathe air. But that wasn't what life was about. *Gott* expected more from His children. He expected them to love and serve one another. It was a commandment, after all. To love your neighbor as yourself. And she loved Ben, no matter how hard she tried not to.

His forehead crinkled. "I will admit when I gave Ben that assignment, I had hoped you two might do well together and decide to marry. Your *onkel* Mervin hoped so, too."

Uh-huh. She'd suspected as much. But it hadn't worked out. Not this time.

She looked away, her face heating up like a torch. "That isn't possible. You know I can't have *kinder*. And Ben wants a *familye* of his own more than anything else in the world. He deserves that. He deserves to be happy."

There, she'd laid it out for him. But surely, he already knew all of this.

"And you don't think he'd be happy with you and no kids?" he asked.

She stared at the baby in her arms. "Would you be happy if you and Sarah didn't have any *kinder*?"

The bishop didn't respond, but she could see him considering her words. Trying to imagine his life without all the sweet children living in his home. It just wasn't acceptable to an Amish man or woman to never have any kids.

"I think Ben would try, but we'd both feel a great emptiness in our hearts," she said. "He'd know it was me keeping him from being a *vadder*. And I don't think I could live with that, even if he could."

The bishop hesitated for several moments, as if thinking this over. Finally, he nodded. "*Allrecht.* I'll do as you ask. But I think you're wrong about Ben. His first love is his *Gott.* I know this, because he's told me so. But love and compassion between a man and woman can conquer a lot of pain we each must face in this life. And if the two of you truly love one another, and trust in the Lord, there isn't anything you can't conquer together."

She stared at him, not knowing how to respond. She longed to believe him but wasn't sure her faith was that strong.

"I'll say good day," he said, tugging on the brim of his black felt hat.

Without another word, he sauntered off. She watched him go, too stunned to speak. Her mind churned with thoughts and strong emotions she didn't understand. Was it possible he was right? Could the love she and Ben shared overcome their inability to have children? She wasn't sure. Not about anything.

It didn't matter now. Ben wouldn't be picking her up for school anymore or hanging around all the time. Bishop Yoder would see to that. And it was probably for the best.

Heaving a big sigh, she wrapped the baby more tightly in her blanket and told herself to stop worrying. As long as Ben was okay, nothing else mattered right now. She must be satisfied with knowing he was alive and recovering. It was enough for her. At least, that was what she told herself.

* * *

"Ben!"

He looked up just as Mary launched herself at him.

"Oof!" He exhaled suddenly as she wrapped her little arms tightly around his chest.

Sitting up in bed, Ben wore a hospital gown and had several thin blankets tucked around his waist and legs. He hugged the girl back but felt a bit awkward when he saw Hannah and Mervin Schwartz standing just inside the door. Seth stood beside them.

"*Hallo!* This is an unexpected surprise," Ben said, feeling a bit immodest without his long-sleeved shirt and other clothes.

"The *kinder* were pretty upset when they heard you were injured. They wanted to come and see that you were all right," Hannah explained.

Seth stepped nearer but didn't speak. Ben had learned that he was a quiet boy who observed everything. It was a mistake to think that just because Seth didn't talk a lot meant he wasn't thinking and feeling emotions.

"Look what I brought for you." Mary held up a picture of a farmyard.

Ben took the paper between two fingers and admired it for a moment. "Did you color this?"

She nodded. "I made it for you, so you can look at it and not be lonely for us while you stay here in the hospital."

He smiled. "*Danke.* I love it. I'll keep it right here beside me until they let me go *heemet.*"

He set the picture on the table next to him, then

looked at Seth. "And how have you been? Taking care of your little sister?"

Seth nodded.

"How was school today?" Ben asked.

"We didn't have school. Everyone in the *Gmay* was worried about you so Teacher Caroline canceled today," Seth said.

Really? That was interesting. They only canceled school for serious emergencies. Maybe he wasn't without friends after all.

He looked up, his gaze searching the wide windows in his room that showed the vacant hallway near the nurses' station. Still wearing his heavy winter coat, Mervin hovered beside the door, holding his black felt hat in his hands.

"Where is Caroline? Is she not here?" Ben asked.

Hannah stood behind Seth and rested one hand on the boy's shoulder. "*Ach*, she's waiting for us outside with the *boppli*. She wanted to be here, but we were told you can only have a few visitors at a time. She thought it would be better for her to let the *kinder* come see you instead."

Hmm. That was interesting, too. Was this Caroline's way of reminding him that she wanted nothing to do with him? Because if that was the case, he wasn't buying it. Not anymore. He'd almost died yesterday, and that experience had changed him somehow. It made him realize a lot of things that he'd been pushing aside for too long.

"You're really okay?" Seth asked quietly, his eyes filled with worry and a bit of suspicion.

Ben nodded. "I'm really okay. You know how doctors are. They like to fuss over you. They're just keeping me here one more night for observation. They want to make sure my lungs are working right and the frostbite is clearing up satisfactorily."

Seth's eyebrows lifted in a curious expression. "Frostbite?"

"*Ja*, they feared I might lose some of my fingers and toes." Ben laughed and waggled his fingers at the boy for emphasis.

"Really? You almost lost your fingers and toes?" the boy asked.

"Some of them. But they're fine now. The doctor just wants to make sure."

Seth smiled. "That's cool."

Ben laughed, thinking it was impossible to keep their Amish children from picking up some of the *Englischers'* language.

Ben hadn't lost any fingers and toes. And what a relief. The situation had been quite serious last night. Alone in his bed, in the quiet of the night, Ben had wept when he thought he was going to lose parts of his body. What would Caroline say if that were to happen? Already, she thought he was a monster because he'd killed a man. He didn't want her to be any more repulsed by him than she already was. But *Gott* had truly blessed him and he was more than grateful. And now he missed Caroline more than ever. Knowing she was all right was all that had kept him focused through the harrowing ordeal he'd suffered last night. But he longed to see her now.

Mervin touched Hannah's arm to signal they should leave. "*Ach*, we don't want to overstay our visit. We'll be going now. We'll check in with the bishop tomorrow to see how you're doing."

"But I don't wanna go yet," Mary whined.

"Me either," Seth said.

"We must, my dears. We need to buy some supplies and get *heemet* before dark. And Ben needs his rest now," Hannah said.

Ben nodded and hugged each child as he offered them a warm smile. "*Danke* for coming. I appreciate it. I'll see you in a few days."

His promise seemed to satisfy Mary and Seth, and they willingly preceded Hannah and Mervin out the door. Ben stared after them, thinking. He'd been told that Caroline was waiting outside.

Bracing a hand against the hospital bed for support, he stood carefully and peered out the window. Sure enough, Caroline stood on the shoveled sidewalk, bouncing baby Susan on her hip. She gazed lovingly at the child and spoke to her before laughing. The baby waved her tiny arms, completely enthralled by the beautiful woman.

Caroline lifted a hand to adjust the little girl's tiny black traveling bonnet. And though Ben couldn't hear her, he could just imagine Caroline's loving words as she tended the baby. In his heart of hearts, he knew Caroline would make the best mother, if only she could have children. How he longed to marry her and make her his own. But it was impossible. She couldn't seem to forgive his past faults.

And then a thought occurred to him. He'd never really asked Caroline if she could forgive him. What if her cool attitude toward him had nothing to do with him

killing a man? What if her actions were simply protec-
tion for herself because she couldn't have babies? To
keep them both from being disappointed?

Hmm. Maybe he'd been completely wrong about
Caroline. It couldn't end like this. Could it? But what
other choice did he have? Maybe it was time they had
a long chat. And maybe he should be prepared to offer
some possible solutions to her concerns.

A plan started to form in his mind—but it might
not work at all. She might still rebuff him. However,
with their future happiness at stake, he had to try one
last time.

Chapter Fifteen

Caroline reached into the metal bucket she held, grasped a handful of grain and flung it low in the air. The chickens scurried forward, pecking at the ground to gobble up pieces of barley, wheat and corn. She skirted a couple of mud puddles, noticing the shadowed sky was clear of clouds today. The sun was just peeking over the eastern mountains. It was early and Aunt Hannah was inside the farmhouse, cooking breakfast. The smell of sausage wafted on the air.

Caroline had best hurry if she didn't want to be late for school. It had been ten days since the accident, and she hadn't seen Ben in all that time. She'd been told that he was home now and doing fine. Of course, they hadn't had church yet. But this weekend they'd have Church Sunday, and she had no doubt he'd be there.

It didn't matter. She'd keep her distance, focusing on the preaching and helping the women lay out the noon meal. She had no reason to even speak to Ben.

She told herself that was how it must be.

The rattle of a buggy coming into the yard drew

her attention. She looked up and her heart immediately sank.

Ben Yoder!

What was he doing here? She thought Bishop Yoder had spoken to him to call him off. For the past week, she'd been driving herself to the schoolhouse with no problems. She'd heard that Rand Henbury had gotten out of the hospital and was home doing fine. Without his truck, he had no way of terrorizing the county roads anymore, even if his father hadn't told him to stop.

Surely, Ben had no business at their farm this early in the morning. She feared he was going to assert his will and try to drive her again. And she dreaded the inevitable confrontation. Because no matter how much she loved him, she must strongly insist he stay away and leave her alone. And that was that.

Uncle Mervin came out of the barn carrying two buckets of frothy white milk. Aunt Hannah came out of the house, wiping her hands on a dish towel.

Caroline almost groaned out loud. She really didn't want an audience right now. Not if she must be rude to Ben. Her entire *familye* adored him. Mary and Seth couldn't get enough of him. And she feared they'd all be upset when she had to tell him off.

To make matters worse, Alice and Levi came from the pigpen and chicken coop. She had no idea where Seth and Mary were. Probably in the barn helping with chores. No doubt they'd show up soon enough. No matter what, she must maintain her temper while firmly getting her point across.

"*Hallo*, Ben!" Uncle Mervin called as he set the buckets of milk on the back porch.

While Ben hopped out of the buggy, Mervin reached up and took hold of the horse's bridle to steady the animal.

"Guder mariye," Ben said, his gaze moving to rest on Caroline.

"It's so *gut* to see you up and about. Will you *komm* into the house for some breakfast with us? It's much too cold out here," Hannah said with a bright face.

Ben smiled, his gaze moving back to Caroline. "I'd like that, but I really need to speak with Caroline alone right now."

His words impacted Caroline like nothing else could. Her legs felt suddenly wobbly, and she wanted to fall to the ground and melt into a puddle right then and there. Anything to avoid a bad confrontation with him. Oh, how she loved him. And she didn't want to hurt his feelings any more than she already had.

"Ach, of course!" Hannah waved at Levi and Alice. *"Komm* inside, *kinder.* Let's leave Ben and Caroline alone."

The children did as asked. Caroline watched as her aunt held the screen door open for them to step inside the toasty kitchen.

"Why don't you go into the barn where it's warm and quiet? You can talk there," Uncle Mervin suggested.

Ben nodded and headed that way, waiting for Caroline to precede him through the wide double doors.

She hesitated, wishing she were anywhere but here. Wishing she didn't have to do this right now. Or ever, for that matter.

"Um, what did you want to talk to me about?" she

asked when he'd pulled the doors closed but left them slightly ajar.

He immediately removed his black felt hat in a gesture of respect. Then he gazed at her, his lips slightly parted, his eyes filled with a moment of confusion and doubt. He looked so endearing, shifting his feet nervously. She would have laughed if the moment hadn't been so serious.

"I don't know where to begin," he said.

"Then don't. Let's just part ways as friends, Ben. Really, we don't need to discuss anything at all. We'll forget this ever happened." She turned and took a step toward the doors but felt his hand on her arm tugging her back.

"Please don't go. There are things I must say. I have to get this out now."

She faced him and he released her arm, standing so close that she could see the golden highlights in his dark eyes. She clasped her hands together in front of her before lifting her chin high in the air. She was resigned to listening politely but being firm about what she would and would not do.

"*Allrecht*. Go ahead. What is it you want to say?" she asked.

He licked his upper lip, betraying his nervousness. "First, I love you, Caroline. I always have, from the very first moment I moved here and saw you sitting in church. Other than my *Gott*, I love you more than anything else in this world."

She closed her eyes, a feeling of weakness and euphoria sweeping over her entire body. Oh, how she'd longed to hear him say these words. And yet, this was the last thing she'd expected.

"Ben, I can't…"

"Wait! Let me finish, please." He spoke softly, insistently, as he held out a hand to stop her from speaking.

Biting down on her tongue, she forced herself to hear him out. She owed him that much.

"You're wrong about me, Caroline. I'm not a violent man. Not really. I have my faults like anyone. Sometimes I lose my temper. But I didn't want to hit Rand Henbury. I don't want to strike anyone. But I'm not perfect. I need Christ's forgiveness every day of my life. And I'm trying to be a better man all the time. For you. But I would never hurt anyone. Never again. I hope you can believe that. I'd never lift a hand to you. Not ever!"

There was such passion in his voice. His eyes were filled with such beseeching that she truly believed him.

"I know that now, Ben. I really do. I'm not afraid of you. In fact, when I'm with you, I feel so calm and safe," she said.

He breathed an audible sigh of relief. "*Gut.* That's how it should be. Your example of faith has taught me to trust in the Lord and accept that I can finally forgive myself for the past. I can let it go and move forward. But I want you by my side. I'd like to buy the Harlin farm and add it to the acreage I already own. We'd have a nice home and barn and live a *gut* life there."

Oh, how grand that sounded. It would almost be the fulfillment of all her dreams.

"I… I can't, Ben. I know you are a *gut*, kind man. That's not the problem here. Not really," she said.

Oh, why did he have to say these things to her now?

It made no difference. It couldn't change anything between them, except to make it worse.

"Then what is it? Why don't you want me? Is it because of what I did? Because I'm responsible for someone's death?" he asked, taking a step toward her.

She took a step back. Not want him? Nothing could be further from the truth. But she couldn't tell him that, or she would be lost forever.

"*Ne*, of course not. I know *Gott* has forgiven you for fighting back. You're so *wundervoll* and I respect you so much for all that you've overcome. But I can't have children, Ben. I can never give you a *familye*. You know that," she said.

He shook his head even before she finished speaking. "That doesn't matter to me. That night when Rand Henbury drove his truck into the river, I thought I might lose you for *gut*. I thought I would die. And when I awoke alive, it changed me forever. It made me realize how precious life is. And I knew then that I must not allow myself to have any more regrets. *Gott* wants us to be happy. We must take a leap of faith and trust in Him. We shouldn't waste any more time worrying that we aren't *gut* enough for each other. We must hold on tight and cherish the life we can have together. I love you, Caroline. I want you to marry me. Please say that you will."

She shook her head. "Oh, Ben. I can't. There would be no sons or daughters for us. We could never have a *familye* of our own. And you would resent me for it. Maybe not now, but later on down the road when we're older. You would come to resent me. And I couldn't live with that. I just couldn't."

A movement at the side of the barn caught Caroline's eye. She glanced over, startled to see that Seth had popped up from behind a bale of hay where he'd been hiding.

"I'll be your *sohn*. I'm an orphan and don't have parents now. I want to be part of your *familye* and live at the Harlin place with you," he said.

Caroline blinked in surprise. She had thought she was alone with Ben, but apparently not.

Ben jerked, startled, when little Mary stepped out from behind a milk barrel. Caroline was about to ask if there were any more children hiding in here but didn't get the chance.

"And I'll be your daughter. We need a *mudder* and a *vadder* and you need *kinder*. Why can't we be your *familye*?" the girl asked.

Before Caroline or Ben could respond, Hannah and Mervin slid one of the heavy doors aside and stepped inside the barn. It was obvious from their eager expressions that the two of them had been eavesdropping.

"I think that would be a *wundervoll* idea," Aunt Hannah exclaimed.

"I do, too," Uncle Mervin said.

Caroline almost laughed. So much for privacy.

"Our home always has room for more, but we are overflowing with *kinder* as it is," Hannah said. "If you and Ben decide to marry, I would agree to let you take Seth and Mary as your very own. And I know Anna and James would highly approve of you living at the Harlin place. It's what they would want you to do."

"And I have no doubt Bishop Yoder would support this idea, too, especially since the *Englisch* social worker has given us her approval to keep the *kinder*," Uncle Mervin added.

Caroline could only stare at all of them, stunned by this very generous offer for a ready-made *familye*. Ben eagerly looked at Caroline, and she saw an abundance of love gleaming in his eyes.

"I'm willing if you are," he said with a satisfied shrug. "I love you, Caroline. Say you'll be mine and make me the happiest man in the world."

She laughed, finally realizing that tears had flooded her eyes. "Do you all mean it? Is this what you really want?"

She looked back and forth between the two children, hardly able to believe this was happening. They each smiled and nodded, and Ben took her hands in his own. For once, she didn't have the willpower to fight him. Not when he offered her the very desire of her heart.

"Well? What do you say?" Ben asked her.

"*Ach*, yes. Yes!" Caroline cried and threw her arms around his neck. She hugged him tightly and found herself being picked up and spun around the room in his arms.

Her aunt and uncle and the two children joined them in a group hug. Excited laughter rang through the air as they made their plans.

"It's already late in the season, but I'm sure we could fit in another wedding before Thanksgiving. Becca Graber and Jesse King are getting married next Tuesday, and we could ask if they'd mind us combining your wedding day with theirs," Aunt Hannah said.

In a small Amish community like theirs, it would be

best if they could have a double celebration. In fact, that was a frequent occurrence at Amish weddings.

"Do you think they'd agree?" Caroline asked.

Hannah waved a hand in the air. "Of course. We'll be helping with the feast anyway, and this way, we can share in the expense. Neither Becca nor Jesse has much money, so I'm guessing they'd be relieved to have us go in with them."

Caroline knew her aunt was right. Though a wedding day was extra special, it was always quite simple for the Amish. Their wedding attire was usually new but just a plain dress like what they wore every day. The biggest part of the event was the meal. Since their people weren't overly wealthy, sharing in the cost and work could benefit each of them. Caroline had no doubt Becca would agree. After all, they had become very close friends.

"Everyone in the *Gmay* is helping with the food. Oh, won't they all be so excited when they hear we're having a double wedding? We have so much to be thankful for this year. But we'll want to clear it with Becca and Jesse first. We'll go right over to Becca's house and propose the idea this very morning and see what she thinks," Aunt Hannah said.

"Yes, we should clear it with Becca first," Caroline agreed.

"And if she has any hesitation at all, we'll just hold your wedding the week after Thanksgiving. It won't be a problem at all. You just leave everything to me," Hannah said.

Caroline nodded, accepting her aunt's enthusiasm with a great deal of peace and joy. She gazed up into the face of the man she loved and found him looking at her with so much devotion she almost couldn't contain it all. And suddenly, the room became very quiet. Out of the corner of her eye, Caroline saw her aunt and uncle as they swept her children out of the barn, giving her and Ben a moment alone.

Her children! How wonderful that sounded to Caroline.

As she stared into Ben's eyes, he kissed her deeply, lovingly. And she let him. For the first time in her life, she cast aside all her reservations and held on tight. Because she realized this moment was all they were guaranteed. They should cling to one another for as long as they could.

A feeling of exquisite joy swept over her. "*Gott* has been so *gut* to us. So kind and generous. He brought us together, such a perfect fit."

"*Ja*, it's true. I love you, sweetheart," Ben whispered against her lips.

"And I love you, my *Liebchen*. More than I can ever say," she returned.

"Do you really mean that?" he asked, his voice filled with disbelief.

"I do. I love you, and I'm not afraid anymore. I look forward to spending the rest of my life proving how much I love you," she said.

As he held her tight, no other words were necessary just now. Their love was all they needed to last a lifetime and beyond.

* * * * *

Dear Reader,

Have you ever felt like you weren't good enough? Or that you had so many failings that you were tempted to give up hope and stop trying? Or maybe you made a bad decision at some point in your life that caused a lot of pain for you and others and you don't think you can ever recover. I think all of us have had feelings like that at one time or another. Life is so hard. But through the Atonement of Jesus Christ, all things are possible. We can become better if we repent, work hard and put our trust and faith in Him.

I hope you enjoy reading this story and I invite you to visit my website at www.LeighBale.com to learn more about my books.

May you find peace in the Lord's words!
Leigh Bale

SPECIAL EXCERPT FROM

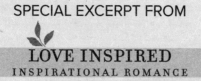

LOVE INSPIRED
INSPIRATIONAL ROMANCE

*When a television reporter must go into hiding,
she finds a haven deep in Amish country.
Could she fall in love with the simple life—
and a certain Amish man?*

Read on for a sneak preview of
The Amish Newcomer *by Patrice Lewis.*

"Isaac, we have a visitor. This is Leah Porte. She's an *Englischer* friend of ours, staying with us a few months. Leah, this is Isaac Sommer."

For a moment Isaac was struck dumb by the newcomer. With her dark hair tamed back under a *kapp*, and her chocolate eyes, he barely noticed the ugly red scar bisecting her right cheek.

Leah stepped forward. "How do you do?"

"Fine, *danke*. Where do you come from?"

"California."

"Please, sit. Both of you." Edith Byler gestured toward the table.

Isaac found himself opposite Leah and gazed at her as the family gathered around the table. When all heads bowed in silence, he found himself praying he could get to know the visitor better.

At once, chatter broke out as the family reached for food.

"We hope you'll have a pleasant stay with us." Ivan Byler scooped corn onto his plate .

"I...I'm not familiar with your day-to-day life." The woman toyed with her fork. "I don't want to be seen as a freeloader."

"What is it you did before you came here?" Ivan asked.

"I was a television journalist," she replied. Isaac saw her touch her wounded cheek and glance toward him. "But after my...my car accident, I couldn't do my job anymore."

LIEXP0820

Journalist! What kind of God-sent coincidence was that? He smiled. "Maybe I should have you write some articles for my magazine."

"Magazine?"

Edith explained, "Isaac started a magazine for Plain people. He uses a computer to create it. The bishop gave him permission."

"An Amish man using a computer?"

"Many *Englischers* have misconceptions of how much technology the *Leit* allows," Ivan intervened. "You won't find computers in our homes, or cell phones. But while we try to live not *of* the world, we still live *in* the world, and sometimes technology is needed to keep our businesses running. So, some bishops have decided a little technology is allowed."

"What's the magazine about?" Leah asked.

"Whatever appeals to Plain people. Farming. Businesses. Land management."

"And you want *me* to write for it?" she asked. "I don't know anything about those topics."

"But that's what a journalist does, ain't so? Learn about new topics," Isaac replied. Her opposition made him more determined. "Besides, you're about to get a crash course while you stay here. Maybe you'll learn something."

"I already said I had no intention of being a freeloader."

He nodded. "*Gut.* Then prove it. You can write me an article about what you learn."

"Sure," she snapped. "How hard could it be?"

He grinned. "You'll find out soon enough."

Don't miss
The Amish Newcomer *by Patrice Lewis,*
available September 2020 wherever
Love Inspired books and ebooks are sold.

LoveInspired.com

pr Michaeli
poly neurogia
rheumatica

LOVE INSPIRED
INSPIRATIONAL ROMANCE

IS LOOKING FOR NEW AUTHORS!

Do you have an idea for an inspirational
contemporary romance book?

Do you enjoy writing faith-based romances about small-town
men and women who overcome challenges and fall in love?

We're looking for new authors for Love Inspired,
and we want to see your story!

Check out our writing guidelines and
submit your Love Inspired manuscript at
Harlequin.com/Submit

CONNECT WITH US AT:
www.LoveInspired.com

Facebook.com/LoveInspiredBooks

Twitter.com/LoveInspiredBks

Facebook.com/groups/HarlequinConnection

LIAUTHORSBPA0820R